THE MIDNIGHT GAMES

David Neil Lee

POPLAR
PRESS

Poplar Press is an imprint of Wolsak and Wynn Publishers, Ltd.

Cover image & design: Rachel Rosen
Interior design: Leigh Kotsilidis
Author photograph: Maureen Cochrane
Resurrection Church of the Ancient Gods logo: Malcolm Lee
Typeset in Garamond & Headline One HPLHS
Printed by Ball Media, Brantford, Canada

The publisher gratefully acknowledges the support of the Canada Council for the Arts, the Ontario Arts Council and the Canada Book Fund.

Poplar Press
280 James Street North
Hamilton, ON
Canada L8R 2L3

The altered lines of poetry in chapter 20 come from William Blake's "Jerusalem."

Library and Archives Canada Cataloguing in Publication

Lee, David, 1952-, author
    The midnight games / David Neil Lee.

ISBN 978-1-894987-96-7 (pbk.)

    I. Title.

PS8623.E436M54 2015   jC813'.6   C2015-903291-1

To Malcolm & Simon

The world is what
you imagine it to be.

PART 1
THE STADIUM

The world is what
you imagine it to be.
Then, something happens.

PROLOGUE

Looking back at that first night, wiser now (I guess) than I was then, I should have said to Dana, "Turn back – let's forget about the whole thing. Because if we don't, terrible things will happen. To you especially."

This is what they call the wisdom of hindsight. We can construct whole fantasy worlds around how things *might* have been … if somehow we had made *that* decision instead of *this* decision. Dana would still be with us, and overall there would have been less fear, fuss and collateral damage. Although Dad and I have never had it all that easy, my life would still be going along in a more or less predictable way.

Or everything might be changed, changed horribly, beyond recognition, and we would all be, if not dead, then thoroughly shafted, and this delicate endangered world that supports us would be doomed. So what if I had kept Dana out of the midnight games, what if I had turned him back, what if we had stayed out of Ivor Wynne Stadium that October night?

"Let's turn back, Dana, because if we don't, terrible things will happen. To you especially," I'd have said. He would have looked up at me surprised, his face pale in the distant glare of the street lights.

Dana had led me to a shadowy corner at the stadium's south end – away from the excited crowd, which I knew from experience was not your standard football crowd, pouring through the front gates: the screaming children and ponytailed women, the men wearing RESURRECTION CHURCH OF THE ANCIENT GODS T-shirts, or baseball caps with the now-familiar logo:

7

According to Dana, we could break into the stadium by somehow, without hacksaws or bolt cutters, severing the steel anchors of its chain-link fence. Here in the shadow of the bleachers, he bent to this task, but if I could do it all over I would say, "Get out of here, man. Out of this neighbourhood, this city. As far away as possible from Hamilton, especially from here in the east end, where dark things and pissheads and evil powers are gathering and scheming to strike at me and tonight, even more so, to strike at you. We're both in great danger ..."

And so on. Then, respecting my new powers of prophecy, Dana would shrug: "Hey man, if you say so." He would fold up his pocket knife and head back to wherever he spent his nights. So even though I will never see him again, even though it means I feel myself missing Dana – who, although technically homeless, had become a part of this beat-up old neighbourhood; I guess I would even call him a friend – for his sake, I'm glad he's gone.

But who am I kidding? It would never happen that way.

Okay – if through some miracle, I'd had this flash of foresight, I would still have needed a lot more in the way of evidence. Otherwise, Dana would have looked up, he might have paused for a second, but he would have just snickered.

"Come off it, Nate. Terrible stuff has happened to me already. Why do you think I got no fixed address?" He would have returned to his work, his thin blade miraculously slicing through the wire anchors. "Terrible stuff still happens to me," he'd say over his shoulder, "on a daily basis. No fixed address for eight freakin' years."

But hindsight is useless, as my dad has always been fond of pointing out. "If I had known then what I know now..." is one of his favourite precursors to an extended reminiscence that is sure to include his constant striving, occasional triumphs, even months and years of being "on a roll," but an admission that if you stood back and looked at the big picture, what you'd see was, basically, failure. He'd prop it up with a conclusion that up to now, I'd always found depressing. "What the heck, you never know." Dad would shrug. "You just hafta keep on keeping on."

I guess at some point or another, terrible things happen to everybody, though some stuff is more terrible than others. Even normal everyday life is often a frightening and dangerous proposition – I'd never thought of it this way before until it was pointed out to me, in person, by the man who claimed to be none other than H. P. Lovecraft himself.

"Nate my boy," he said sombrely. "As I've written, the oldest and strongest emotion of mankind is fear, and the oldest and strongest kind of fear ..."

But I'm getting ahead of myself. Let me tell you how all this started.

CHAPTER 1
SOMETHING HAPPENS

Here in the east end, it's nothing new to see a rundown European church – Polish, Ukrainian, Italian – suddenly turn Asian, its faded signs freshly painted over in Korean or Vietnamese. Along Barton Street, everything from Satan to cannabis has its house of worship. In this neighbourhood, churches loudly promise everything from cancer cures to "glorious rapture" (better, I guess, than the regular rapture). They are just a few of the many enterprises that explode into life, like aliens from a more cheerful planet, cleaning and painting the empty storefronts, putting up a brave face for months or years, waiting for their offerings to catch on, their sparkly display windows gradually turning dull and dusty, before eventually turning off the lights for good, covering the windows with a fresh set of newspapers and heading home.

The first I saw of the Resurrection Church was graffiti: a few words hovering around a logo that looked different every time I saw it drawn with magic marker or brush or spray can. Sometimes it looked like a math problem, sometimes like some weird musical notation, sometimes like a single staring eye.

THEY RETURN!

Just this past summer, on a hot day down by the railway tracks, I had been searching for praying mantises with my friend Sam Shirazi. We had gone down to the end of Markle Avenue, just off the rarely used train line that curved through our neighbourhood into the north end; a no man's land of belching chimneys (mostly gone cold) and vast catwalked factories and crumbling parking lots. Markle led to an abandoned chain factory in the corner of an empty parking lot ringed by dusty underbrush. Behind it, rusted metal smokestacks from an old incinerator still stood – barely stood, it looked to me, getting rustier every year. But that day, the old brick building was showing some action. There were cars parked there, and a sign over the logo proclaimed this as the Resurrection Church of the Ancient Gods.

"Funny place for a church," I said.

Sam responded, "There's a guy in there looking at us."

"We're not on their property. We've got every right to be here."

"Now he's talking to that other guy. Let's get out of here."

"Who cares?" I said. "They look like redneck losers."

"Nate. Yeah," Sam replied.

Sam knows more than I do about run-ins with rednecks. I conceded and we headed back down the tracks. My dad's family is Portuguese and my mom, as I recall her, was some kind of blonde, so I look more or less white-bread Canadian. But sometimes Sam gets a hard time from the guys at school who run in gangs and sneer and bully and, when they figure they can get away with it, punch out anyone outside the gang. At first I'd thought it might be both funny and instructive to point out their feeble knowledge of geography, since they call Sam "Paki" even though he and his family are from Iran. In reality, these mini-seminars were never appreciated. Now I simply try to avoid such confrontations, though when they happen, I stand by Sam. Of course, Sam's full first name is Osama, which doesn't help.

Anyway, I'd thought no more of the Resurrection Church of the Ancient Gods. Until tonight.

"HOLD THIS…" Dana handed me the flashlight. In its uncertain beam I saw him pull out his pocket knife. It wasn't much of a knife, with a rubber handle and a blade about five centimetres long, but this little blade, amazingly, sliced through the solid metal bands that anchored the fence to the fencepost, in this shadowy corner of the chain-link barrier that separated Ivor Wynne Stadium from the city around it.

"Buddy set this up here so he could sneak into Ticats games, he's a big fan. Then a couple weeks ago he asked me – same as you did, Nate – if I knew anything about these midnight games. I didn't know what he was talking about. He said he'd go to one of them and tell me what goes down. But I never saw him again."

"He went into a midnight game, and he didn't come out?"

"Before the game I'd see him every morning buying his smokes at the Big Bee. Every day, seven a.m. like clockwork. Next thing you know, he's gone."

Then Dana showed me his secret. Looking around, he pulled two plastic zip ties out of his jacket. He slipped the bands he had just cut – which weren't metal at all, just zip ties – into a pocket.

"I spray paint 'em silver," he said proudly.

At that moment a roar blossomed from the crowd and the announcer's excited voice – "ON THE WAY, THE GREAT ONE HIMSELF" – blasted from the stadium's sound system. "Go go go quick quick quick," Dana urged me, pushing the fence's lower corner inward and following after I scuttled through. From the shelter of a dumpster we could just see the football field's illuminated east end. Dana gestured at the nearest refreshment booth. "Nate, buy a beer," he whispered. "So we won't look like total moochers. Get an extra cup."

"I can't buy a beer. I'm underage."

"The way I hear it, tonight anything goes. This is a *midnight* game. I'll meet you back here."

"But ..." I was going to say "... they know me here." Dana had already faded back into the shadows. I worked the stadium concessions during football games in the summer and fall. I have made a lot of hot dogs and been hissed at by a lot of drunks, but I'd picked up a few cooking skills, and probably social skills too.

As it happened, I didn't know the bartender, who wasn't much older than me and looked unsurprised when I materialized out of the shadows in the black pants and hoodie that Dana had recommended and which I usually wear anyway. When I held up one finger he poured a Steely Dan into a plastic cup without asking for ID. I pushed the money toward him. I was only sixteen and didn't look a day older, but Dana had said that at midnight games, anything goes. Well, we would see.

"Could I get an extra cup?" I asked. "My buddy's has got a crack in it." He pulled a cup from a stack.

"Good crowd tonight," I observed.

"More all the time, and we got something real good this week," the bartender said. "Yog-Sauces will be smackin' his lips when he lands here." He turned as a new group of customers approached, laughing and slapping and jostling each other excitedly.

I retreated to find Dana had closed up the gap in the fence, and was waving to me from just inside the nearest entrance, looking out at the lights on the field. He pulled a Steely Dan of his own from his pocket and emptied the can into my offered cup.

"No way I'm buyin' it here," he said. "It's five bucks a beer, isn't it?"

"Six." That six bucks had hurt and I was hoping Dana would at least split it. Actually, I had been hoping this evening would be free of charge. At least now we looked like legitimate paying customers. We started up the stairs to the nearest bleacher, the beer sloshing in its plastic cups.

FOR ALL the noise the midnight games made, with their thunderous announcements and heavy metal music pounding through the neighbourhood, tonight there were no more than a few thousand people here, filling the lower rows of the bleachers, watching the bright lights and the figures running and scattering and feverishly prepping the field below. Dana and I had agreed that, to stay inconspicuous, we would head for the empty upper tiers where we could look down on the crowd and scope out whatever was going on.

My father and I live two blocks away from the stadium, on the other side of my old school, the boarded-up Prince of Wales Elementary that we preferred to call PoW. This was the house I grew up in, an old three-storey brick house that my mom and dad had bought to raise a family, though they'd only managed to produce me before my mother died ten years ago, when I was six.

Since the summer's end, once every week or ten days, the games had been keeping our neighbourhood awake. Everyone on our street was used to Ticat nights, when the blasts of music, the amplified chanting, the flyovers by jet fighters and antique bombers, the blasts of cheering were all tolerable because they were part of our way of life, and because they finished by ten p.m.

I had inherited my father's lack of interest in football, but since I'd turned fifteen, and began to work in the concessions, I'd welcomed the games and even enjoyed the noise and the drunkenness, the anticipation, the bursts of excitement. Like a lot of kids in the neighbourhood it was my first real job where I made real money. Not only did I make some money, but for a few hours a new world opened up, a world different enough from mine to make me happy to clean up the spilled drinks and grease spatters, fill up on leftover fries and hot dogs, and leave the custodians to dim the lights as I left the stadium and went back to everyday life.

But I didn't know anyone who had ever been called to work the midnight games. I could have used the money, but when I called the concession they had nothing for me. "Those are private contracts."

I didn't mind too much; there was something weird about these games, not advertised online or on the radio, unreported on TV or in the sports pages. They started up at midnight, when the streets filled with families and couples and crowds, hollow eyed and obsessed, bickering and swearing and trading lines from songs I'd never heard, as they came from all over the city to converge on the latest Midnight Game.

"The guy at the bar mentioned something called Yog-Sauce," I said, "or Yog-Sauces." I fought for balance as I skidded on a wet spot.

This was another reason to keep going up, and up; the occupied seats were awash in Steely Dan. It turned out I had been alone in my pathetic purchase of a single beer with extra cup. The customers who were arriving as I left had taken trays to handle all the beer they needed, and among the crowd plastic cups slopped Steely Dan across plastic seats. People were noisy and excited: "Get this show on the road," someone yelled.

We passed a baby in its stroller, shrieking and ignored while its mother, a ponytailed woman spilling out of her shirt, screeched at the man in the baseball cap next to her. "I wanna be a cougar. Why? Because cougars are awesome. Because I wanna find a loser like you and chew his leg off!"

"I haddit with you!" he shouted. The baby kept crying. Dana and I, keeping our heads down, trudged up the steps to the upper tiers, our shadowed feet crunching through discarded empties and splashing through puddles. Halfway up the section we started to find empty rows; and finally we sat down on benches above the crowd. I sipped my beer. The benches were damp with dew, or what I hoped was dew, drawn out of the air as the autumn night cooled.

"This beer tastes funny," I observed. Dana was squinting out at the field.

"They done something with the team colours."

"Not that I'm an expert. My dad says that Steely Dan is made from diet ginger ale and rubbing alcohol."

Dana wasn't listening. As music boomed from the speakers I looked down into the glare on the field. Sure enough whoever was playing wasn't wearing the Ticat black and gold. At the west end of the field the team was dressed all in black and at the opposite end, the team was in white. White, I wondered, how do they do it? The grass stains must be hell to get out. I pulled out my phone and clicked a few photos.

Different music started playing, some big booming orchestra thing. A whistle blew, the teams started to run. They weren't wearing helmets or any other gear or padding. I blinked hard against the field lights. What kind of moves were these? Precise and practised, but bizarre. The black and white ranks moved together, then shifted to make points and angles and corners, forming strange, unreadable patterns. It was not football at all, but some kind of weird flash mob or performance art, sending messages best seen from above, messages not to the crowd in the bleachers but to the night sky itself.

Once again I tried to tackle my beer like a man. I didn't want to give up, especially having invested six bucks. But the next time I took a sip, I spit it out. "I can't drink this beer," I told Dana.

Dana ignored me, his gaze on the field below. "There's no ball," he said.

I shoved my almost-full cup under the bench. The period, or dance, or ceremony, whatever it was ended and cheerleaders poured out onto the field. Instead of cheering and chanting, the crowd fell dead silent and, as one body, rose to their feet. Dana and I looked at each other. We stood up too.

Now the competing teams merged in the middle of the field, and through their ranks came four players, carrying between them a long, wrapped bundle on a kind of stretcher. By the time they reached the centre, a huge square of black tarp had been laid out on the turf. From our seats in the upper tiers I could barely make out the network of lines and angles that decorated the black square. But when I squinted at those lines, trying to see them better, my vision seemed to blur. I blinked: what was going on?

Someone in the crowd began to sing, and gradually more voices joined in.

"I'm a worker and I wonder
When I'm gonna hear that call of old

My old hometown's goin' under
All the furnaces gone cold

"I'll be reachin' out to heaven
Where cuhthooloo reigns supreme
When his ancient city's risen
I'll be livin' in a dream."

And as those lines were repeated, other voices sang against them: "Yog-Sauces Yog-Sauces Yog-Sauces." I didn't know what the heck the song was about, but the crowd had sung this before. Whatever you call it, the effect when you sing different musical parts against each other like that, it was eerie, but beautiful. "Yog-Sauces Yog-Sauces ..." I started joining in; Dana looked surprised but soon, to keep up appearances, he started moving his mouth in time with the others. I kept repeating my part; it needed work; *Yog* was no problem, but there was something funny about the way they were pronouncing *Sauces*. I wasn't quite getting it right. Did everybody here have a lisp but me?

"All these years I've kept on hopin'
That a change is in the wind
And someday soon the sky will open
To let the old gods rule again."

I felt a tingling like an electric shock. I looked around. Where was it coming from? There were no hidden wires. Low clouds, thick and slithery as smoke from an oil fire, roiled around the upper reaches of the stadium and I wondered about lightning.

Suddenly I heard someone speak into my ear; a voice deep, vibrant and reassuring: *I can help you.*

I looked around – there was no one was except Dana. I shivered. Was I having a psychic experience? Was this literally the excitement of the crowd, somehow transmitted through the thickening atmosphere around me, filling me with notions? What was going on? From school assemblies, sporting events and fairs I knew that a crowd was a place where a lot of people get excited over stuff that any one of them, if left on their own, would see was hopelessly dumb. Was that what was happening to me?

The shrouded stretcher was carried out onto the black square and laid pointing east to west; the performers stepping back so we could all have a good look. Then the cover was whipped off and I gasped.

On the stretcher lay a naked man. He was one hundred per cent ordinary looking, a pudgy guy in his forties with dark hair and short legs. Blindfolded, his hands and feet bound with duct tape, he shivered and tried to rise, but fell back. I wondered if he had been drugged with something. Numbly I raised my phone and took a few more pictures.

"What the hell is going on here?" asked Dana. Everyone else just kept on singing. As the chant thundered over the public address system I felt the structure under me shudder as if, in the depths of the stadium, something huge was rising to the music.

Now a line of men in overalls came shambling out onto the field. Shambling and awkward, because each of them had a heavy barbecue-style propane tank on his back, with a long hose and a nozzle.

They were carrying tiger torches. I was familiar with these, in a way, because for three or four birthdays, when I was a kid, I had asked my dad for one. Watching road crews softening asphalt, I'd decided that a tiger torch was the closest thing I'd seen to a flame-thrower – which, as I'd learned from watching *Them!* with my dad, was the best weapon to have in case giant ants appeared. But Dad never got me one.

Someone on the field was gesturing at them to hurry, and they lit their torches and lined up on either side of the stadium entrance directly below Dana and me. Raising the nozzles before them like heraldic trumpets, they formed an avenue of flame leading to the man on the tarp.

Above the chant of the audience I could hear a roaring and humming in the air, as if the sleeping sky itself was waking up, rumbling and hungry. The noise grew in volume and when it swelled, the concrete stadium itself began to vibrate. I could still pick out a few of the announcer's words. "HE'S COMING… HE'S COMING… HE'S COMING."

I wondered if the Steely Dan I'd sipped had not just been a crummy beer, or skunky, but if there was something seriously wrong with it. I couldn't focus my eyes on the glare above that square of black tarp. The air above the spiky symbols and the naked man seemed to glow, like gasses in a fluorescent tube coming alive with an invisible charge. And I could feel an excitement myself, something I'd never felt before, like a voice inside me saying, *I can help you, I can save you, and the hell with everyone else, you are a winner. You are a winner and you will overcome. You will overcome and there is a god that will lead you. A god will lead you, and I am that god, and the name of that god…*

On the field below, the line of flames wavered, and suddenly something enormous clattered and shook its way out of the entrance beneath us and moved into the field; something as long as a bus, with bony limbs and feelers waving and shuddering. I blinked to see better, but the light over the stadium was strobing and flickering. The people around us waved and danced like cut-up movie frames, and I could see the shape move toward the man on the tarp, lunging and feinting at the line of flames that held it back.

The performers moved back, and the shape paused. It reared up over the naked man, who was trying frantically to break his bonds and get away, sensing the danger nearby. He began to shout, words I couldn't make out in the racket around me.

"… POWER SOURCE," the voice boomed over the sound system. "AND IF WE JUST TRY A LITTLE BIT HARDER… C'MON, JUST A LITTLE MORE! … THIS TIME HE'LL COME. THE ENERGIES ARE HERE … WHEN THE EXANIMATOR FEASTS ON THE ENERGY FROM THIS TWO-FACED COWARD WHO TRIED TO STOP US, THIS TRAITOR, THIS TERRORIST …"

The creature pounced and snapped the naked man into its jaws, effortlessly lifting him from the stretcher. He screamed, and for a moment the crowd fell silent, then burst into cheers as the creature turned, carrying its victim – I could now see it had long prickly feelers, or antennae, and two compound eyes like an insect – and surged back through the line of torches and disappeared under the stadium.

"… IS GONE !!!" The crowd cheered. "AND HIS SUFFER-ING, HIS SACRIFICE, WILL GIVE US THE ENERGY WE NEED, THE PUSH TO PROSPER, THE WILL TO WIN …"

The darkness snarled and rumbled like an earthquake shaking heaven itself. There was a spark of lightning, and like fog before a storm a wall of blue smoke blew across the field. High above us, something black and red and monstrous tore through the gathering clouds and thrust its way into the halo of spotlights. A cry went up from the crowd, a cry of ecstasy, and shooting from my toes to the crown of my head I felt a shock of fear as if I was teetering on a high roof, at the edge of a deadly fall. I cried out and then reeled back as a vast presence – outlined with luminous globes, writhing against the field's glow and with the glint of a gleaming hungry eye – took shape before me. I was panting from the excitement, from the thrill of that voice, from the strange urge for glory and triumph that had run through me like a shock, and I shook my head to clear it.

Then the darkness sparked brilliantly again, before the glow began to diffuse and fade into the night. The tarp on the turf lay in a heap, crumpled and stained with blood.

CHAPTER 2
SOMETHING FOLLOWING

You would probably think Dana was a pathetic character unless you shared a neighbourhood with him. But after he'd been on the street a while, people noticed that he didn't harass anybody for spare change, that he wasn't scoping out porch furniture or lawn tools to steal and that he would pay attention if you spoke to him. As my dad liked to say, if you have no money, people don't respect you, but as the years go by and you still have no money, you get credit just for still being around. Dad was talking about himself, but the same thing applied to Dana.

Every week, we would see Dana cruising down the street on garbage day, starting in the afternoon when some of our neighbours first put out their trash, then again after supper, when more blue boxes were put out. Finally, he'd go by late in the evening, to catch those people who put out their trash just before bed. Each time, he'd rifle through the blue boxes for bottles and cans, and throw them into a big duffle bag he had slung across his back. He didn't talk to anyone unless they said, "How ya doin'," or insisted on cornering him in conversation, so he was pretty much accepted. Although Mrs. Smot, the lady Dad called "Betty Bylaw," always squinted at him suspiciously, and the odd guy who'd had a bad day would toss an insult.

I got to know Dana a couple of years ago, when I decided to start running. A few times a week I would get up early – I was self-conscious and didn't want anyone to see me, so I only did this before the sun was up – and run for a few shadowy kilometres. I would cut through the Prince of Wales' schoolyard and run around the stadium a few times, or cross Cannon to do laps on the grass around Scott Park if the ground wasn't all mucky, or even run all the way down to Gage Park and back.

One morning, in March, still dark, I opened the door and jumped when I saw a shadow move on our front step. It was Dana, with a pocket flashlight hanging around his neck. Our *Hamilton Spectator* was unfolded on his lap and he was doing the crossword.

"Jeez." He started frantically erasing.

I was still woozy from sleep. Before this, I'd not taken much notice of Dana when I'd see him on the street and, with his scraggly hair and his old clothes, I had simply figured him for one of the street people who are always coming and going. But for a street person, if that's what he was, he looked pretty clean and he didn't have that glassy-eyed crackhead look. I stood staring for a minute. Then, since it was my front porch after all, I did my best to take charge.

"Do you do this every morning?"

"Sorry, man." He'd finished erasing. "Yeah, I just do them lightly, with this." He held up a mechanical pencil. "Then I erase 'em good."

"What a weird thing to do."

He scooped up his duffle bag from the porch. "You surprised me today." And then our paper was back sitting on the porch, neatly folded with the elastic band around it, the same way I always found it, and Dana was gone.

"Now that I think about it," I told my dad later, "sometimes I've wondered why there are eraser shavings in the GO section."

"Who does this guy think he is?" Dad asked.

"Dad, it's not as if you or I even do the crossword."

"We pay for that darn paper."

Shortly afterwards I started taking the crosswords page of the GO section, once I'd finished reading the comics, and leaving it under the green box on the porch. After that, every morning when I opened the front door, the page from the previous day was gone. From that point on, Dana and I were in some way friends.

He told me a little bit about life on the streets. "It's been getting stranger the last couple of years."

To me, it seemed like a life of adventure: Dana lived from hand to mouth, carrying all his possessions in a leather satchel and a big old canvas backpack, yet for all that he was a free man. In the warm weather he could sleep anywhere, having become highly skilled, so he told me, at making shelters from a plastic tarp strung over branches or old lumber. In the winter he prowled the old industrial district at the north end of the city. He liked it, he said, because so much of it was empty. But it wasn't as empty as it used to be.

"Maybe the steelmaking is picking up?" I said. "More traffic?"

"It's not that," Dana said. "At night, up in those territories, you'd swear the world had ended. Nothing but weeds and rust and broken windows. Except for me, even street people don't go up there; it's too far away from everything. But it's not deserted like it used to be. I get a funny feeling, and I hear things. I go there at night, and sometimes I get a glimpse …" He paused.

"Glimpse of what?"

"Nothing I guess, just shadows, and movement out of the corner of your eye. And I hear things. Last winter, walking along a railroad track I'd walked on a hundred times before, something followed me."

"Something?"

"I dunno, but I could hear it in the bush, just behind me, moving when I moved, stopping when I stopped. Freaked me out."

"Maybe just a raccoon or a coyote," I said. "Anyway, you're still here." But now Dana was off in his own world, this other Hamilton I knew nothing about.

"There's an old freighter down there – the *Sandoval* – I've been using it for years, off and on, climbing up onto the deck and pulling up my gear with a rope. It's been sitting there in the harbour so long even the rats have moved out, but I get my candles going and make it snug…"

"It sounds pretty sweet," I said. "Maybe some night I could …"

"… but then again … last winter, with the ice thick around the ship, at night I heard something …"

"Out on the ice?"

"No – *under* the ship. Something that came out of the lake, something big. I could hear its back rubbing against the hull, and all night I could hear water surging, and the ice cracking, with whatever it was doing down there."

"So ... what could that be?" I asked. "A carp, or ...?"

"Nate, I mean *huge*. When it bobbed against the hull, the whole ship rocked. In the morning I saw where, under the ice, it had come and gone. There was a bloom of mud spreading out into the bay. Something big comes out of the deep part of the lake to tunnel under the city, and it comes at night, and it uses the old freighter for cover."

"Jeez ..." I didn't know what to say, except that Dana, already an unusual friend as friends go, was starting to sound a bit nuts.

"Something is happening, Nate," Dana said, and he blinked and was back in the city, the sunlight, the traffic, the present moment. "Things are changing."

"Maybe it's a change for the better," I said. I know, a lame thing to say. To be honest, I was starting to change my mind about joining Dana, even temporarily, in his vagabond life of freedom and adventure.

"Whatever it is, I gotta stay out of its way," Dana said. "Otherwise, one way or another, I know I'm gonna get screwed."

CHAPTER 3
SOMETHING BESTOWED

I stared down at the chaos on the field. The announcer, himself disappointed by the turn of events – whatever they had been – changed his sales pitch. "… PROUD TO BE A MEMBER OF THE RESURRECTION CHURCH OF THE ANCIENT GODS … YOUR DEVOTION … YOUR DONATIONS … TONIGHT WE CAME SO CLOSE … IN JUST A FEW DAYS …"

"What just happened?" I asked Dana. I was clicking through the pictures on my cellphone. But the action on the field, the man on the stretcher, the shape in the sky, the creature that had seized its victim and vanished – everything had been too dark and too far away.

In practical terms, Dana gave me the best answer I could hope for: "Let's get the hell out of here."

The crowd began to chant again. This time there was a different melody along with the words, a melody I recognized from hearing it spilling over from the games through our neighbourhood late at night. "… the dark clouds come again… from the sky a magic … our furnaces will blaze… the stars above … the Great Old Ones draw near…"

Whatever these ceremonies were all about, whatever was bringing these people together, whatever bizarre nation was coming together here, I guess this was its anthem.

"Hurry up." I grabbed my beer from under the bench, and suddenly Dana was leading me down the steps past the cheering crowd. As we approached the landing, I saw a dark figure coming up. Leaning against the steel rails, turning to look up at the bleachers illuminated by the flashing lights from the playing field, was a tall white man, I guess in his late thirties or forties, perfectly dressed in a dark business suit. In the glare of the lights, his eyes glimmered against the silhouette of his face like flares on the dark side of the moon. He looked sharply at Dana as he hurried past and then turned to look at me.

"Hey," he said and then louder, "hey, you don't belong here."

He stepped in front of me and our eyes met. He was an eerily normal-looking guy, with undistinguished features and one of those waxy, too-perfect hairdos you see on politicians and old-time movie stars.

"No pictures. Everyone knows that."

"'Scuse me." I tried to go around him.

"No pictures. You wait right here," he grabbed my arm and threw me off balance.

I poured my beer down the front of his pants.

"Hey!" Horrified, his grip loosened and I pulled away. Dana's head appeared in the stairway, hissing at me to hurry and as this guy – Mr. Slick, I thought of him – recoiled from me, his shirt front and pants dripping with cold Steely Dan, I ducked and followed Dana down the concrete stairways dimmed with smoke from the games.

"Gatecrashers," I heard Mr. Slick cry out behind us. "Gatecrashers here! I've been assaulted!"

Dana headed for the corner where we'd come in, but I grabbed his arm. I'd seen a familiar face. I rushed up to a guard at the nearest entrance, a girl I'd gone to PoW with, and who I knew from working the concessions. Like me, Kara had started cooking hot dogs, but unlike me, apparently she had moved up in the organization.

"Nate!" Kara was my age, a tall dark-haired girl a bit on the heavy side. She gave me a big smile. "Didn't expect you here!"

"Hey, Kara – look, can we get out this way?"

"Great ceremony tonight, eh? Big changes coming!" She turned her head, distracted by the shouting behind us. A crowd was gathering around the joint in the fence where Dana had gotten us in; there was no escape that way.

"Look, Kara, I gotta get home… Can we…"

"We almost got him through tonight, didn't we? Jeez, Nate, I thought I heard the Proprietor... did he just call a lockdown?" Kara looked back into the crowd to see what the fuss was about.

"Thanks, Kara..." I slipped past her and through the gates, Dana right behind me... "You're the best, awesome ..."

Out on Balsam Street, we began to circle the stadium to head back to my place. As we came around the front we merged into the crowd pouring from the gates. Now I felt safe.

"So, Dana," I said. "What did we just see in there?"

"That poor bastard on the stretcher." I had never seen Dana look this upset, but I couldn't blame him. "Something *snatched* that guy."

"Next time the big one," came a woman's voice from the crowd.

"The next game," someone else said, "the boss'll be here, and our troubles'll be over."

"We'll finally have a goddamn boss who's on our goddamn side for a goddamn change."

"We can't let them do this," Dana insisted as we worked through the crowd. He turned and shouted, "ANY BLOOD SPILLED AT IVOR WYNNE – IT BETTER BE FROM FOOTBALL!"

"Jeez, Dana." I grabbed his arm. "Let's just go home. We can call the cops."

"And they will do what?"

I looked around, but no one seemed to have noticed Dana's outburst. It felt like we were safely lost in the crowd. Figures were spilling out of the stadium into the dark street, but they weren't pursuing us – just heading home themselves after the latest midnight game.

Then suddenly he was right in front of us. Someone grabbed me from behind and Mr. Slick put a hand on my shoulder. A hand cold as if the night itself had reached out and stopped me in my tracks.

"Getcher hands off him," Dana said. I could see other figures in the crowd, rising to join Mr. Slick. I felt a hand reach into the pocket of my hoodie and grab my phone. I struggled but my arms were pinned. Once again Mr. Slick looked into my eyes.

"Hey, this is a public street here," I said. "You got no right to stop me."

"I'm the Proprietor," he said calmly. "And you're the boy who dumped his beer all over me."

"That was an accident," I lied. Then I lied again. "I'm sorry," I said. "Give me my phone back."

"You *are* just a boy," the Proprietor said. "I can even see some potential in you. Here ..." Suspicious, I kept my eyes on his face even as I reached out and took the business card he handed me.

"But you..." he turned to Dana. "We've been watching you. You should mind your own business. Here's a little something." He handed Dana a slip of folded white paper, like the tickets we photocopy for school events. "It's your future," the Proprietor said.

Dana looked at the Proprietor, took the paper, grabbed me and pulled me away from whoever was hanging onto me.

"My phone," I said. I turned to see a darker-skinned man, no taller than me but built like a bulldozer, holding it. He was clicking through my pictures, deleting as he scanned them.

"There's nothing here anyway, sir," he said. "The light was so bad, and this is a real piece a crap." He made as if he was going to throw my phone over the fence, back onto the stadium asphalt.

"Hey!" I was ready to grab my phone, no matter what it took, but the Proprietor turned and paused, looking surprised. A bulky figure on an electric scooter had pushed through the crowd, saying something to him that I couldn't catch.

"I had to do it," the Proprietor sounded annoyed. "It's his future, or a whole world just waiting for us, that's what's at stake." The person on the scooter answered him back, posing questions in a laboured, wheezing voice. I couldn't hear the words at all, and only caught snatches of the Proprietor's reply: "... none of your business ... takeover ... don't need your opinion ... the *dritch*, it's a wild animal, it acts of its own free will ..."

He turned and stomped toward me, sending one last

comment back at the person on the scooter. "I don't want to hear 'sorcerer,' the sorcerer is not a factor." He shook his head in disgust. "Everybody around here thinks my business is their goddamn business."

This was obviously my new bud's number one problem. I would keep that in mind.

He looked back at me. "Jimmy, give him the phone." Jimmy tossed it on the pavement in front of me and I scrambled to grab it.

Not giving us, or anyone else, another glance, the Proprietor and his followers strode off, the crowd parting at their approach. The watchers around us turned away, but a whisper seemed to follow us – "future, future, future…" – as Dana and I threaded our way through the crowd to the open streets. By the time we got to Lottridge we were on our own. I was testing my phone; I could get a dial tone, and the camera still worked. I turned to Dana.

"Jeez, what in the world … what was that all about?"

Dana shook his head. "It's not like life isn't strange enough already."

"What was that thing? We just saw a guy on a stretcher get served up to some monster."

"Unless those were like, you know, projections, or holograms."

"No way. It was right there in front of us. A centipede-type thing as big as a dinosaur. It came out from under the stadium. It ate that guy."

Dana shrugged. Somewhere behind us, from a crowd heading up toward Barton from the stadium, came a cheer and a snatch of song. "SOMEDAY SOON THE SKY WILL OPEN …"

"They had all those torches," I continued. "You don't need a wall of fire to control a hologram."

"…show business …" Dana said vaguely.

"And that voice in my head. I heard a voice in my head. Did you hear that? Telling me I was the greatest, and that together we'd defeat our enemies and rule the world."

This seemed to perk Dana up a bit. "Yeah, I heard that too. I didn't believe it ..."

"Me neither."

"... but it was powerful. You could feel how you could get taken in by something like that."

"My dad calls me a natural skeptic," I boasted.

"If I believed all the lines people feed me," Dana said, "I'd be dying, dead or in jail."

"I saw something too. Slithering through those clouds, like a snake, but it was huge, and glowing ..."

"I need to get outta here," Dana said. "Reboot my brain."

I couldn't help him with that. We were silent for a moment, then I thought of what the Proprietor had handed to Dana. "What'd he pass you?" I asked.

For a second Dana didn't seem to understand. Then he reached into his pocket and pulled out the slip of paper. He unfolded it and spun around to the nearest street light. Dana scratched his chin. "I was hoping he'd slipped me a twenty," he joked, "but this ..."

Along the slip of paper someone had drawn a line of stick figures, like some kind of rough cave painting. Within these figures, sharp angles stood out, black and forbidding, against the white paper, pointed and final as the corners of a swastika. They were just symbols, or ancient letters or pictures or something, but when I looked at them I shuddered. Then on impulse, I held up my phone and took a picture.

"Forty-two hours..." Dana read.

"You can read this? Is this lettering?"

"It's written right there." He pointed. "Right at the top." He squinted.

"I don't see..." If Dana was reading something there in English, I sure couldn't see it.

"It was there a second ago," Dana held the paper up to his eyes. "'In memoriam Dana Laschelles allowed forty-two hours.' I saw it right there. I read it. Just a second ago. Now I don't see it. Go figure."

"Do you mind if I take that?" I asked. "I can search some of this stuff online. Maybe it's a code."

"I saw it right there." Dana seemed about to give the paper to me, then he shook his head. "I'm gonna hang onto it." He looked at the streets around us, now empty and dark, as he said, "It's not yours, Nate. It's for me."

I was headed home to a house that was nothing fancy, but at least the lights worked and the heat was on and the front door locked up with a key. I didn't know where Dana was staying.

"Look, Dana, why not crash at my place."

In the past, though I knew it might not make my dad happy, I'd asked Dana to come and stay; we had lots of room and he could take a shower, do some laundry. But he'd always refused. The east end, he told me, was full of abandoned buildings. There was always someplace he could get in and make a squat, at least for a while.

Lately I'd brought the subject up with Dad and he hadn't been a hundred per cent negative.

"We've got these bedrooms," he said, "and once he has an address, he can at least get welfare, and probably even a job." Dad's eyes had brightened. "We could charge him rent ..."

I turned to Dana one last time.

"Are you sure you don't want to ...?" But we had just passed the abandoned school, and Dana was gone.

CHAPTER 4
SOMETHING SCUTTLING

When I was little, I loved the old Tarzan movies that Dad brought home from his store, with Johnny Weissmuller fighting crocodiles and lions, discovering lost cities and rescuing the good explorers, all while punishing ivory hunters, evil chieftains, criminals and Nazis. In those movies, Tarzan lived high in a jungle plateau called the escarpment.

I remember how scared I was, when I was about five and heard my mother and a friend plan a hike up the escarpment.

"D'you think I can bring Nate?"

"Sure – it's a long way up, but if he gets tired ..."

"NO!" I ran away and had to be coaxed out from under the basement stairs. Often as it figured in my dreams, I believed that the escarpment was guarded by great apes who dropped boulders on unwanted explorers. In the movie, the visiting safari had been doomed until Tarzan showed up – and I knew that Tarzan was fiction, even if the escarpment wasn't.

My mother explained to me that the escarpment was simply the Niagara Escarpment – that great tree-covered cliff to the south that you can see from everywhere in our neighbourhood, which everyone just calls the Mountain. When I finished at Prince of Wales, my counsellor recommended that I go to a school up on the Mountain that had programs better suited to students like me, who, because they get good marks, are saddled with that godawful label, "gifted."

Now I ride the bus up and down the Mountain every school day, eyeing the thick covering of trees, the blasted walls of ancient rock, peering for a glimpse of the secrets behind them. I was always thinking and wondering and never giving up hope that, just behind the boring routines of everyday life, there might be something really interesting.

My whole neighbourhood was built early in the twentieth century, when the steel industry was booming and people were coming from all over, mostly Europe, for the jobs. My dad tells me the houses around here are cheap; we all have backyards maybe six metres wide and ten deep, fenced off from each other with old pipe and chain-link fences.

The northeast corner of our yard is a bamboo thicket. My dad said he and my mom had planted a potted bamboo there when I was a baby: "We had no idea it would grow like that." I didn't mind; when I was little I would make forts in that bamboo. It is evidently a semi-tropical plant, but it likes it here by the lake, where the air stinks of sulphur and ozone during the long steamy summers. The bamboo grows like an enormous weed; in spring I bring out a stepladder and trim the tops with long-handled clippers to stop them butting into the hydro wires.

THE MORNING after Dana and I crashed the midnight game, I got out of bed and stumbled into the bathroom. Something fast and furtive was scuttling, whispering around the bathtub, climbing the side and falling, climbing and falling. It was one of the big house centipedes that sometimes fall into the bathtub at night, or slip out of a wall and skitter around the floors, hiding under rugs and inside books. They are fast and gross-looking with their long legs and feelers, but I've gotten used to them. They scoot here and scoot there, in fact I looked them up and their Latin name is *scutigera. Scutigera coleoptrata.*

Creepy as they might be, I don't like squishing living things. I took the empty peanut butter jar I kept on my bookshelf, scooped up this creature, popped on the lid and took it out to the backyard. Still in my pyjamas, I took the lid off of the composter and unscrewed the jar. The centipede shivered on the bottom, every part of it alert: its tiny black compound eyes, its feelers, its fifteen pairs of legs trembling and ready to flee me or fight me. It wasn't happy about leaving our warm house. But the compost heap would offer it new adventures, lots of new little critters to eat; maybe it would even survive the winter.

"Hey, scooty," I said. "Here's to new worlds."

I upended the jar and watched the centipede hit a blackened banana peel and skitter off into the muck of onion skins, eggshells and apple cores.

I looked back at the jar: something still moved, flexing and stretching ambitiously. The centipede had left a leg behind, closing and extending all on its own. But the bug hadn't seemed to miss it as it happily ran off into the compost. I guess with that many legs, you don't limp if you lose just one. I blew into the jar to dislodge the leg and shook it, still bending and flexing, away into the grass. A big black-and-white cat tiptoed over and sniffed at it.

"Don't think you want to eat that, Pips." Pips wasn't our cat; too fat and glossy to be a stray, we figured that he lived somewhere, with somebody, in the neighbourhood. But he liked our backyard. Dad, for whatever reason, started calling him Pips. We didn't know what his owners called him.

Before I went back inside, I checked out my amazing bamboo stump. I crouched over it, balancing gingerly so I wouldn't fall onto my knees in the dirt.

Bamboo, I knew from experience, puts out underground shoots; a few shoots, pointed as arrowheads, came up in our yard every spring. In fact, Dad had me dig ditches in that corner of the garden and embed hunks of sheet metal in the ground in an (unsuccessful) attempt to stop the runners from snaking under the fences into the neighbours' yards. Still, every summer the lawnmower slashed hunks of bamboo shoots out of our backyard's embattled grass.

Over this past summer, our patch had birthed the Godzilla of all bamboo shoots. I'd found it in August, when it had obviously just broken through the soil – its rounded shape was dirtied with chunks of moist dirt – and it was already as big around as a coffee can. Now, two months later, it was thick as a hydro pole and, when I poked it, felt just as solid. For sure Dad would want me to chop this up and cover it over.

But I kind of liked this stump. It looked to me like one of a kind. It obviously had a will of its own; even now, as the fall advanced and everything else was pale and withering, Stumpy was growing and thriving. The weather had been dry lately; I got the garden hose and gave the stump a good dowsing.

Pips came up next to me and sniffed at it, flicking back and forth his long black tail with its white tip. Even he could tell there was something different about Stumpy. Then something rustled in the weeds, and Pips turned and bounded away.

I looked up and saw a black shape flickering behind the bamboo that screened our back fence. I walked over to the fence, eyeing the house behind us for movement in the windows. The lady there didn't like me petting Rocky.

Rocky jumped up on the fence and thrust his stinky face into mine. He's a big bony black Lab crossed with something else; maybe Rottweiler, since his head is wide and flattened, like a salamander. He used to bark at us a lot, so one day I told Dad I was going to make Rocky into a project.

"Take it slow," Dad had said. "Not just with that dog. Melanie's got a hell of a temper: don't get her mad at us, and don't get yourself bit."

"There's my buddy," I said, scratching Rocky's big ugly head. "There's my big boy." I reached into a pocket and pulled out a marrow bone I'd scooped from the kitchen. I flicked it into the air and, quick as a frog snapping up a fly, Rocky caught it with a crunch. I flicked him another one, and another, but I was running out of time and soon I headed back inside.

CHAPTER 5
SOMETHING BIG

Early in the morning, when I don't want to get up, I project myself; or imagine that I do. I picture myself as a set of eyes with no body, flying eyes or a spirit or a disembodied brain or a ghost that hums and hovers and drifts here and there like a humming-bird over every wall and yard and through the streets of this beat-up old city, the only city I know.

I can launch off the lip of the Mountain, the rock face a hundred metres high that separates the new city from the old – launch so convincingly that, although I'm lying there in bed, I get a rush of vertigo as I fly, flicking leaves from the tops of the trees that anchor the crumbling soil of the cliffs. Then I skip off the roof of a freight car lumbering along the railroad line that follows the foot of the escarpment, and fly up Sherman Street past blocks and blocks of brick houses covered with soot from the few remaining factories that belch out smoke in the dead of night. I soar through the bedrooms of workers – slow to rise, like me, this time of day – the kitchens of hardworking mums slurping Pepsi to get them out the door after their too-short nights Steely Dan and Lakeport on their back porches to get them to sleep at the end of their too-long days. I buzz through the downtown criss-crossed with moving bodies and buses and cars and wheelchairs and electric scooters to the empty houses and warehouses of the north end. They are full of ghosts, my neighbour Ronny tells me, ghosts who worked and sweated and dreamed of something better, but who still ended up ghosts. This is their abode: the crack houses and the dazed women with smeared makeup who stand wobbling on street corners at seven in the morning. I go past the banked flames of the few coke ovens still simmering; past the lineups at the morning food banks; the SUVs and the oversized pickups of the guys with steady jobs and Ticats season tickets. I can zoom past them all quickly, through their yards and windows and kitchens so fast with my imaginary flying eyes because I fly silent and invisible and …

"Hello, Nate? Excuse us – *Mr. Silva*!"

I sat up and blinked and tried to look surprised. *What? Me? Sleeping?* Everyone had a big laugh.

"I hope we're not making too much noise for you, Nate."

I mouthed something about being up late, but everyone just groaned at my lameness. It was not first thing in the morning, but 11:15 a.m. and I was not in bed, but slumped over my desk in English class. When it was over I tried to avoid Mr. Delmonico, but he intercepted me.

"Seriously, Nate," he said. "You like English. You've never nodded off like this. What's going on?"

"Have you ever heard of the Resurrection Church of the Ancient Gods?"

Mr. Delmonico nodded. "Those people? I thought they faded away years ago."

"They're back."

He shrugged. "They were one of those little hot-dog cults who get going for a while, rope in a bunch of followers for a few years, and then fade away. Didn't they make a big fuss down your way a while back, at the stadium? There was a fire, or an explosion …?"

"I don't know about that," I said. "But they're holding ceremonies in the stadium late at night, making a big racket."

"You can call the city on them. There're bylaws about that sort of thing."

I hesitated to tell Mr. Delmonico more. I was afraid that if I told him what I'd seen, he would sign me up for drug counselling.

I yawned. "People claim that they've called bylaw, but nobody ever comes."

"You can always call the cops," he said. "I'll call them myself. I can't have some fast-talking cult keeping my best students up all night."

"I've got to get to science class."

"The Resurrection Church of the Ancient Gods. I really thought they were gone for good." Mr. Delmonico shook his head. "They were tackier than the Scientologists."

I WAS still smarting with embarrassment when I got on the bus after school. I looked glumly out the window as we reached the lip of the Mountain and started down. The few roads, choked with traffic, that led up and down the escarpment were a lot like my life up to this point. On every side was interesting stuff – the fringes of old forests, still supporting raccoons and woodchucks and a thousand species of plants, bugs and other critters; waterfalls; layers of rock that spelled out eons of geological time, all part of that mystery world, the escarpment. But here I was, day after day, riding the bus up and down this same narrow, paved strip, with no time for that other world, bored and wishing and thinking about all the other stuff I might do someday. The adults around me were always talking about having high hopes for the future, but they themselves seemed buried up to their necks in the past, with the classic rock and their Ticats sweaters and their nostalgia for the great days of the steel mills. Different worlds – which world did I belong to?

I WAS thinking about this when I got off the bus and walked over to the old Prince of Wales Elementary. I took a good look at it. The workmen, gradually taking it to pieces, were gone for the day. Unable to cut through the fenced-off playground, I skirted it by going down to Cannon. There, a small group of city workers in hard hats and fluorescent vests were probing a big sinkhole that had swallowed up half the sidewalk. I leaned over and peered into the darkness.

"Stay back there, sir!" The "sir" yelled like an insult. A burly guy with black hair curling out from under his hard hat came up to me. "C'mon, kid, get back."

"What the heck is this?" I asked.

He shrugged. "They're popping up all over the place."

"But what causes it?"

"I dunno, we can't figure it. Usually heavy rain, floods. But we haven't had anything like that. Could be seismic activity."

That could be true; over the summer, once or twice I'd felt the house rock as if a dump truck had run into the front porch; and a few weeks ago in the school cafeteria the light fixtures had trembled, and a ripple had radiated through the surface of my chicken soup.

"But even regular earth tremors don't cause *this*; most of the shock is absorbed through the soil and rocks. This is different –"

"Maybe it's a volcano," I joked.

"Right," he nodded. "I saw that movie." (So had I of course – about a million times.) "Wouldn't it be our luck? A goddamn volcano in the middle of Hamilton – just when real estate is going up." He yelled at his buddies. "Kid says it's a volcano!"

A few of the guys guffawed and one of them told me to shove it. The burly guy scratched his head. "I dunno about that, man. It's more like there's something big down there, and it wants to come up. Maybe it's some old First Nations' god that's pissed off …" He gestured me away. "But you really got to stay back. No telling what these things will do."

I LEFT him and his buddies to their sinkhole and kept on circling the school, taking a close look at the plywood over the ground-floor windows. On the Melrose Avenue side, right under the Reserved sign where the principal used to park her car, I found what I was looking for: a plywood sheet where half the fasteners were screw heads, not nailheads.

Dana had told me that he did this at abandoned buildings, late at night when no one was around. With a few tools he carried in his duffle bag, he'd pry loose the end of a sheet and pull out the nails. Then he'd go inside, screw in a hook and eye so he could pull the end of the sheet closed against the window, spread out his sleeping bag and stay the night. His favourite sites were buildings recently closed for demolition: "water's still running, toilets working, I bring the shampoo – it's like a night at the Sheraton!" Before sunrise he'd rouse himself and leave the way he came, fastening the plywood with screws instead of nails. The following night, he'd be back to unscrew them…

"… and I'm home for the night – luxury accommodation!"

It was those screws that told me that this, for sure, was Dana's latest squat … his home until the roof was peeled off and the walls trucked away, until there was no more shelter inside and then he would find another place – coming back to scope out the prospects when a new Prince of Wales Elementary School began to rise to replace the old.

CHAPTER 6
SOMETHING ARISES

My detour past the school had made me late getting home. Dad had been called in for an evening shift, so he'd started supper early. In the morning I had pulled out some noodles, planning to make pesto, since I'd bought sauce and some walnuts (cheaper than pine nuts).

When I had started school up on the Mountain, I'd been one of three boys who had taken Family Studies. I had the idea I needed to learn more about cooking, since Dad did most of our grocery shopping at Dollarama, and I felt I was missing something. I took the course and got interested in cooking from scratch.

Also, some of my friends ate food that I thought was really good. At Sam's house, for example, they fed me dishes with vegetables and grains I had never heard of. Another friend's dad was good with quick stir-fries. Even Dana, to an enough-already extent, had lectured me about the importance of diet in successful homelessness.

But today, I was too late. Dad had defaulted to his standard spaghetti with canned meat sauce. He'd started without me, eating quickly with one eye on the clock.

"Where you been?" he asked me between mouthfuls.

"I was just over looking at PoW. It's all boarded up."

"That was a good school," he said. "They did all right by you."

I served myself at the stove. "They'll be back. They're getting a whole new building." I did not share Dad's nostalgia for my elementary school days.

"Didn't hear you come in last night," Dad said.

I sat down across from him. "Let me ask you." I rolled up some noodles and watched the strands slide off the fork and droop lazily back to the plate. "Do you know what all this noise is, over at the stadium at night – you know, these midnight games?"

Dad sighed. "They've been making a racket lately, haven't they? More active than they've been in a long time." He gave me an anxious smile. "For years now it's been the same: they start up, people complain, they get shut down."

"So you've never been to one yourself?"

He shook his head. "Never been a sports fan. Besides, I was so busy with the business back then – the last time the midnight games were really going – working ten a.m. to eleven p.m. ...."

"Of course," I sighed. Dad had operated Touchdown Video at King and Gage back at the height of the video rentals business. He was doing so well that when my Uncle Don convinced him to invest in a Woodstock start-up – a little company that was making computer desks – he felt he was on the brink of big-time financial success. But the desk business went belly up, and when Touchdown Video had to finish switching over from VHS tapes to DVDs, Dad didn't have the money to make the change. I'd heard this story many times, and I was hoping I wouldn't hear it again now.

"Besides," he said, "it's probably some kind of, you know, ethnic thing – I dunno, a soccer club from one of those little African countries. Bet they get a good rate, using the stadium that time of night." He looked at the clock. "At least with the weather getting cold, soon we'll be shutting all the windows and won't hear them."

"Dana and I snuck into the game last night."

I waited for his reply, hearing in my head everything Dad would say when in an anti-Dana mood, those downtimes when he feared that, instead of broadening my perspective on class struggle, Dana would encourage me to quit school and hit the streets, living out of my backpack and trailing shopping bags and lost toys like so many of the homeless. *You did WHAT? Was Dana stoned? You're lucky you didn't get arrested! Is he doing crystal meth?*

Why does a smart kid like you buddy up with a guy like that?

But Dad didn't say anything. There was, in fact, silence. His spaghetti saw its chance and slid silently back onto his plate.

"The thing is, Dad, it's not a game at all. It's some kind of mass ritual thing. We even saw…"

"Stay away from the midnight games."

"That's what I'm saying, Dad. They're not games…"

"Nate, I know what they are." His voice was getting quieter.

"But you just said…"

"I lied. If you get mixed up with that Cuhthooloo cult …"

I was still getting used to that word, first hearing it chanted by the crowd at the game.

"Cthoolhu," I said, experimenting with the sound. Dad thought I was correcting him, which he hated.

"Thoolhu, Cuhthooloo, for pity's sake, Nate. They've been around for years. They flash lights and blow smoke and talk about bringing back the so-called old gods –" Dad waved his fork in the air as he made scare quotes with his fingers "– but they don't do anything but suck people in and take their money…"

"No kidding …" I started to complain about the price of beer, then thought better of it.

"… and eventually run them down to nothing and then dump them like trash. They appeal to all the down-and-outs in this town, the people who gave everything they had to the mills, and then got left high and dry when free trade came in and the steelmaking went offshore. The Church tells them that with the Great Old Ones in charge, the furnaces will start up again and they'll be sittin' pretty. They'll all have speedboats and cottages and season tickets …"

"Dad, let me just ask you…" I wanted to know what he thought about the human sacrifice we'd seen. Was that just lights and smoke? If Dad knew so much about the Resurrection Church – I was hearing stuff from him I'd never heard – maybe he could set my mind at rest about that. If I could just get a word in edgewise.

"…and gas will be cheap again, and they won't have to worry about pollution or global warming and everything will go back like it was in the 1950s. If they just bow down."

"So, Dad, let me just ask you …"

"Nate, all that is lies, lies set up to suck in weak and scared people – people who are scared because times are hard, they're poor and getting poorer and they'll turn to any god or false god or con man or fast talker. You better not have anything to do with that so-called church."

"Dad, I'm not joining them. I was curious, but jeez, it looked like someone got killed last night, in some, I dunno, ritual or something." I described it to him as well as I could. "I've never seen anything like it. The sky above the field was vibrating, like it had come to life. And then …"

Again, I almost told him about the thing that had clambered out of the bowels of the stadium, snatched that man off the stretcher, and vanished back into the darkness. I mean, it wasn't something that I would believe, if I hadn't seen it.

Even as he raved at me about the Church, Dad kept glancing through the kitchen door, where he could see the clock on the stove. "Look, I've got to go to work," he said. "But first I'm going to tell you something I've never told you."

He was agitated, but I knew my father would have to get hit by a truck before he'd be late for a shift at the department store. I wasn't one hundred per cent sure he would be late if *I* got hit by a truck. I offered to walk him to the bus. By now the sun was low in the sky, leaves changing colour on the few trees left in the neighbourhood. A light haze softened the outline of the distant escarpment. We walked down the street, Dad looking to every side, tilting his head toward me so he wouldn't have to raise his voice.

"Your mother… she got so lonely living here… I'm not saying she wasn't a good mother, she was the best. She thought you were the greatest thing that ever happened. But you know, she was from out west, and she never got used to life here in Hamilton, and she got sucked in by that Church, by their promise of a better world. Though if you ask me, it'd be a world where we'd all be slaves, we'd be fodder, for those monsters. Yog-Sothoth. Cthulhu. Meet the new boss —"

We turned the corner onto Cannon, and a breeze arose from the south end of the stadium. Low clouds darkened the sun and I shivered and zipped up my hoodie. We watched for the bus to appear and take my father downtown, where he could transfer up to the Mountain.

"– same as the old boss," Dad continued, "only worse. But your mom was slipping out to these Church meetings ... at first they were in little rented halls and church basements and off-nights at bars. Then it began – the crowds got bigger, the music started up, the so-called midnight games started up at the stadium. Your mother was excited about this. I was disgusted by the whole thing, but I let her go her own way, hoping she'd get bored and come back to us, but one night she slipped out and didn't come back."

He looked down Cannon Street. Cars came around the curve toward us, varying in shape and colour but perfectly paced in their speed and formation, like a flock of geese. Dad was choosing his words carefully.

"Then they hit their peak, the games – the last round, ten years ago, before they started up again this summer. I never should have let her go. Somebody brought in some kind of a bomb. That's what the papers said – an 'explosion of undetermined origin.'"

"You always said it was a car accident."

"Her, and several other people – seven altogether, the cops told me. There was a lot of ... a lot of damage. They didn't let me identify her body – it had been a thermal explosive, they said. A lot of the bodies were unrecognizable. They found this." He took out his keys and shook them until a wedding ring appeared among them, tarnished silver and black with most of the gold burned away.

"I searched high and low for any evidence about what drew her to the Church, about what she thought she would accomplish. The funny thing is, before she left that last night, she'd wiped her computer. When I booted it up, the hard drive was empty. And there was nothing written down. No names or numbers or addresses. Those bastards wiped her off the face of the earth, and it looked like she'd done her best to help them."

I barely remember my mother, and over the years I'd gotten pissed off at her for dying so soon, as if she'd just gotten sick of me and left. I knew that wasn't fair, but Dad's story brought back all those feelings. My mother sounded self-centred, crazy and wrapped up in herself and the Church.

"You always said it was a car accident."

"Nate, you were so little. And I didn't really know the whole story anyway." He shrugged. "Never will know, I guess. I'm sorry."

"Why did she delete all the data off her computer? Sounds to me like she was trying to cover something up. Like she meant to take off anyway."

"Don't ever say that," Dad growled. "If you ask me, she was protecting me and you. Especially you." Another formation of cars passed and now the bus appeared, grinding its way around the curve from Gage.

"Protecting us from what?"

"Stay away from that Church," he said brusquely. The bus pulled up to the corner. "I can't have that goddamn Church taking everyone away from me." The door swung shut and he was gone.

CHAPTER 7
SOMETHING MALIGN

It took a few minutes for my old desktop computer to boot up. But I checked the modem, and at least our internet was working. I started a search: what, I asked Google, were "yog sauces"? It didn't sound like a nickname for a new street drug. I scrolled through pages of results without finding anything useful. I found entries for yogourt sauces, and sites where yoga shared space with recipes for peanut and tahini sauces. I was on the wrong track, I thought. Chances were slim that the crowd in the stadium had been chanting about their favourite yogourt. Then, as if reading my mind, an entry caught my attention. "Yog-Sothoth," it read cheerily, "is not yogurt sauce." I clicked through to the site and read:

> YOG-SOTHOTH is the eldest and most powerful of the Great Old Ones who are redoubling their assaults on our world as the twenty-first century progresses. Yog-Sothoth's appearance is uncertain – those who have seen it range in their reactions from devotion, to revulsion, to incurable lifelong madness. Even Lovecraft himself was vague, in one work referring to Yog-Sothoth as "only a congeries of iridescent globes, yet stupendous in its malign suggestiveness."

Who was this Lovecraft? The name was linked so I clicked again and found stuff about Howard Phillips Lovecraft. Some early twentieth-century American guy who wrote horror stories. Back to Yog-Sothoth, where I read:

The keys that will admit the Great Old Ones – spoken and written spells, chemical potions and rituals of human sacrifice – are encoded in the *Necronomicon,* a book written in AD 730 by the Persian writer (although he is often referred to as "the Mad Arab") Abdul Alhazred.

Hmm … if these people know about Yog-Sothoth, crazy as all this stuff was, maybe they knew something pertinent to my situation. The website was called The Lovecraft Underground. On the About Us page I found a mission statement:

Since H. P. Lovecraft's untimely death in 1937, there has been a growing area of study into what has been called the Cthulhu Mythos – research that has uncovered evidence of substantial truth underlying work that was formerly considered fiction. Starting in 1946 with rumours of the ill-fated Nazi space probe *Oberth A-7,* continuing in 1952 with Jacques Cousteau's abandoned expedition to the Indian Ocean trench he called *le fond condamné* and buttressed by the controversial 1967 photographs from the Rocky Mountains' infamous Valley of Bones, a small group of researchers, working independently of university, institutional or government affiliations, began to assemble a body of evidence that Lovecraft's fictions of an ancient extraterrestrial race – The Great Old Ones – trying to restore its earthly domain were based in fact.

To their growing horror, these researchers concluded that they had discovered a danger to life on earth that needed to be researched and made known to the public at large, a danger that needed to be stopped at all costs. Above all, at a time of crisis an alarm must be raised to expose the secret workings of the Great Old Ones on Earth. With this in mind, in 1974 the Lovecraft Underground (LUG) was formed.

I clicked until I found a Contact Us page, and sent a message. *Here in Hamilton, Ontario, we are experiencing an unusual phenomenon. Every couple of weeks the local football stadium puts on late night "midnight games." But the people who come to these games don't seem to be football fans.*

I began the next sentence several times *I snuck into one of these...* then changed it to *A friend of mine snuck into ...* but grew more worried and settled on *I ran into someone,* implying a stranger who, if anyone asked, could stay safely anonymous and unavailable.

... who attended one of these games. He was confused, but he had the impression the games are some kind of mass cult ceremony in which they call on a god named Yog-Sothoth, and where one or more victims have possibly come to harm. Can you tell me anything about this? Is this the kind of stuff your Underground investigates?

I read and reread the message. I wasn't sure these were people I wanted to get to know. But what if I didn't follow this up? Would last night go away? Would that creepy Proprietor guy go away? Would the midnight games go away? And what about that writhing shape in the sky, and the voice that in one way was reassuring, but in another way scared the crap out of me?

I filled out the form with my name and email, even my cellphone number, ignored the invitation to Like us on Facebook, and clicked Send.

CHAPTER 8
SOMETHING DREAMED

I am not big, as sixteen-year-olds go. There are guys in my grade, lots of them, who are a foot taller and a hundred pounds heavier. I wouldn't want an extra hundred pounds (not unless I was awesomely buff, which most of these guys are not), but I can't see a downside to gaining an extra foot of height. If I joined the Resurrection Church, would Yog-Sothoth grant me a growth spurt? I wouldn't bet on it.

In the past, being smallish set me up for a certain amount of bullying; my strategy was to get good at escaping and running fast. Lately though, the bullying had eased off. So by and large things at school are pretty good, except for the odd psycho like the mountainous Tyrone Gunn-Trojak; but Gunn-Trojak moves slowly and you would not call him a subtle type of dude. It's always easy to see him coming. But escaping, in my opinion, is still a worthwhile talent; to maintain and enhance this ability is one reason that I keep trying to get in shape, though I think I need more self-discipline.

That night in the stadium, compelling as the voice was, I remained skeptical. As Dad had preached to me more than once, if something seems too good to be true, then it probably is, et cetera, et cetera, but still I could not get that voice out of my head. This all swirled through my mind as I tried to fall asleep. I dozed and awoke, dozed and awoke, and finally I sent my mind exploring.

I know it's all imagination, but I feel sometimes that I really am leaving my body and projecting my mind out to other places. I thought of the sinkhole on Cannon Street, pushed psychic fingers into its dirt and gravel floor, felt it grind and shift and send up plumes of dust as vast muscular forces pushed upwards from deep under the earth. I circled PoW – yup, I could tell Dana was in there. Like me, he was tossing and turning, lying awake and then dozing off, under siege by strange dreams. I crossed the street to the stadium, and sent my mind into the field entrance where we'd seen that bizarre creature emerge to take its human sacrifice. I got inside the door, but could go no farther. Why not? If this was all imagination, why couldn't I imagine *that*?

"Nate?"

I was inside the corridor where the creature had emerged and the darkness ahead of me was too dense, some kind of super darkness made up of time and space, and memories dense and heavy as a wall of steel. I swivelled to see a woman's figure outlined against the stadium entrance. The stadium lights were on; there were people out there and I could hear music and shouting.

"Nate?" The woman's voice was calm. "I've got to go. They've summoned the exanimator."

I moved closer. This was how I remembered her: untidy hair, black boots, a scuffed leather handbag, a jean jacket with pockets that ... well I remembered that between her handbag and her jacket pockets, she seemed like she could conjure up just about anything.

"There's only one chance," she said. I was drawing closer and closer. "That's the sorcerer, but I can't leave you, I can't ..." Going faster and faster, I lunged toward her, but I plunged right through her and was out on the field. There was shouting and gunshots. Looming over the stadium, the black clouds shot with red lightning that I had seen during the midnight game. And looming over me was that creature, its segmented body raising and turning to reach me, its mandibles clicking eagerly, dripping with venom. And I fast-forwarded out of there, my mind's eye hovering high over the chaos in the stands, looking back to see the creature – *exanimator* – turning toward the stadium entrance, seeing the ghost who'd seemed to be my mother standing there. But losing all will, I slammed into the night air, away from the stadium, over PoW (where outside the doctored shuttered window, I saw a huddled figure hurriedly screwing the plywood back in place), back down Somerset Avenue …

I bolted up in bed, panting and sweating. I looked at the clock. Nate, I thought, you are due for a run.

I changed and exited the front door to find I wasn't the only one having a restless night.

Dana barely looked up when he heard me come out. "Hey, man. Seven-letter word for *sea bass*?"

I shook my head and sat down beside him. "I didn't think you did this anymore. Not since we've been leaving the crossword under the green box."

Now he looked up. "I've done them all. Jeez, Nate, I've had the worst sleep since that night at the game. I dream about the ceremony, and that big shape we saw in the clouds, and that guy, and that – that *thing*, whatever. And hearing voices chanting. Yog-something, fahengluey something cthulhu … just stupid, I know, but that cult stuff really gets to you."

What? This sounded just the tiniest bit like my own dream. But that was goofy.

"And I feel like I'm being … ah, forget it." Dana blinked and shook his head. "I've looked some of this stuff up at the library. They've got a book there in their special collections. The *Necronomicon*."

"Try *grouper*," I said. "But – they've got a *Necronomicon*? I just read about that online. It's ancient – hundreds of years old. The library's got one?"

"I guess it's a reprint. But still, they keep it locked up. You need to fill out a form to look at it. I did that yesterday morning, but then I went in again late last night, 'cause the weirdest thing happened …" He carefully wrote GROUPER into the puzzle but then let the paper fall onto his lap.

"Dana?"

"The words and the pictures … they blurred on the page … and I thought I smelled smoke, that burnt-wiring smell of that

52

blue smoke we saw at the ceremony. And I couldn't read the words. Nothing made sense."

"Dana, enough is enough. Let's talk to my dad about you moving into our house. There's empty rooms."

He looked at me. "'In memoriam Dana Laschelles allowed forty-two hours,'" he said. "Tonight, that time will be up."

"Dana, you're freaking me out. Maybe you shouldn't do this street stuff anymore."

"If the book can't help me, nothing can. I'm screwed."

"This is nuts. Think you've got a fever or something?"

"The voices, and the smells," he said, "and out of the corner of my eyes, I see movement, things are shadowing me. Watching me ..."

"It's like you told me, being homeless is hard work. Maybe it's getting to you. Come crash with us. Even my dad says if you had a place to live you could get welfare, get a job."

Dana ignored me. "There've been things tucked away for a long time," he said. "Hiding and waiting. Now they're coming back."

"It would be win-win." I stood up. "Are you even listening?" With just a sweatshirt and track pants on, I was getting cold.

Dana stood up too. "Let's talk about this. Tomorrow." He scooped up his backpack, full of his provisions for everyday life, tarps and candles and hand tools. Hanging off the back, the pair of absurd pointed-toed shoes. "Don't pay attention to me, I get anxious, I'm just mouthing off."

"Well, stop it. Remember, I rely on you to be my role model." We had joked about this before, but now it sounded awkward. "I'm going for a run," I said and started to jog toward Lottridge. "See you later."

"And hey, man," Dana called, before I passed out of earshot, "thanks for you know ... everything."

CHAPTER 9
SOMETHING STOLEN

"Who might you side with?"

The words echoed past me as I walked toward the library's York Boulevard entrance. I didn't pay them any mind, thinking I was overhearing someone else's conversation. Behind me I could hear the growing hum of an e-bike. Without looking, I moved to one side; there are lots of e-bikes and electric wheelchairs in downtown Hamilton and some of those people drive like hell.

"The Proprietor – he gave you a push?"

This time I turned around. It was a huge woman perched on an electric scooter. Beneath a stained cloth cap she had streaked, wispy-looking grey hair, and a round face with red cheeks and a droopy chin. From the neck down what struck me was not the mishmash of old clothes that swaddled her body; it was how big that body was. Beneath her arms it spread lumpy and shapeless, drooping over the edge of the scooter on both sides, her legs hidden by a drab, billowing skirt.

I gave her lots of room, but she didn't pass. She pulled abreast of me and kept pace as I walked. "You talking to me?" I asked.

"He said you had potential. I could hear him. You saw me there?" Now I remembered. In the crowd outside the stadium, a figure on a scooter having words with the creepy guy called the Proprietor. "Don't you think there's a time to take sides? If we don't act, there will be suffering, people will be eliminated. They have never been this close: the Great Old Ones."

"Take sides? I don't think so." I eyed the library doors. I could get there in ten steps, but they seemed a mile away. "Whatever's going on, I don't really think it's up to me. You know, I really have to …"

"They want this so much. Doesn't your friend fear, now that he's been passed the bad angles?"

I sighed. I hate it when strangers try to recruit me for their politics or their religion, or because they think I might have some money on me, or because they think I'm cute and they want to buy me an ice cream. Dad has counselled me to be polite, but firm, but today I had a lot on my mind. I didn't see why Dana's well-being was any of this lady's business. "I'm sure he'll be fine," I said. I started to move away.

"He has no time. For him, you need to choose. The time is uprising. The exanimators have spread and are rising from below. You must beware the exanimators; even the Proprietor fears exanimators. More than all the rest, beware the Hounds."

Examinator ... or exanimator ... where had I heard that word? The woman's accent, or the way she used her words, was odd. It was a bit like talking to our neighbour Reg, who'd had a stroke: sometimes you had to fill in the blanks. What was an exanimator – did she mean an examination, or an examiner of some kind? And who or what were these hounds? The only hound I knew was Rocky. Dana had been handed a slip of paper, not a "bad angle."

Speaking of bits of paper, she was scribbling on one. She tried to hand it to me. "I am here," she said, "to give you advice."

That was it for me. I laughed out loud, ran the ten steps and ducked into the library, shaking my head. When I looked back, to my relief, the scooter lady was putting the paper into one of her many pockets, and buzzing away across the street.

"I WISH we'd never acquired this stupid book."

I had spent a lot of time in the central branch of the Hamilton Public Library, but I had never visited Local History & Archives, where they told me the rare books were kept. The librarian who had taken my order form was not the one who actually fetched it. "I'm just going on break," she'd said, "but Meghan will bring this out for you."

Meghan was tall and broad shouldered. Her face and her carefully streaked blonde hair were rather plain, but I noticed that as she strode across the library floor, with her black suit and her long legs, everybody raised their heads. She looked at me severely and flicked her purple scarf as she plopped the book on the desk in front of me and made her complaint about "this stupid book."

"Fascinating," I said. "A book-hating librarian."

Meghan refused to smile.

"I haven't been here that long, but they tell me that the most popular books here are requested once every two or three years. Lately, we get asked for this one once or twice a week. It's non-circulating – it can't leave this room – but someone always tries to walk out with it. I've had to call security on some of these people – last week I grabbed it back from a guy myself." She glared at me. "I warn you, do not try that."

I handed her my library card. "I'm just doing research."

She snorted. "That's what they all say."

"Look, *Meghan*, I just want to take this book, *Meghan*, and sit down at that table over there, *Meghan*, and look at it. I thought you were supposed to help me do that."

Snorting again, she scanned my card and gave it back. Then she walked me to the far corner of the farthest table from the door and plopped the *Necronomicon* onto the table.

"You can sit here and look at it," she said, "but you can only handle it with these." She handed me a pair of thin white cotton gloves. "When you're done, you can return it to me, or whoever's at the desk."

"Thank you, Meghan."

"Just don't mark the book or try to walk out with it. I've had it with you people."

The feeling was definitely mutual. I was glad when she turned and left me there with the book.

I sat and looked down at the cover. The cotton gloves hardly seemed necessary. This was no ancient calfskin tome with dusty pages of vellum, or papyrus, or whatever they used to print books on, but a sturdy paperback. It looked well-used, but its laminated cover and dog-eared pages were not, by any means, about to crumble beneath my touch. The title page was still a bright white.

The Annotated Necronomicon, eds. Aldiss and Wilson, London: Saliva Tree Editions, 1971.

On the next page some kind of demon with a tentacled mouth stared up at me, drawn in ominous Gustave Doré–style with deep inky blacks.

I HEARD voices and looked up. At the main desk, Meghan was fielding questions from two people. I recognized them from the night at the stadium: a tall, muscular white woman with a buzz cut, and a shorter, pudgy man who looked Indian or South Asian. He was the guy who had grabbed me outside the stadium and messed with my phone. They both wore plain white shirts and dark slacks, like the prowling evangelists who hassle me at bus stops with their pamphlets and Bible stories.

"… not familiar with that title," Meghan was giving them the same attitude she'd given me. But what would she do next? For a second she glanced at me and I raised my hands and shook my head. *Don't put these people onto me!*

She turned her eyes back to them. "I'll look it up for you."

"You know perfectly well what we want." The woman began raising her voice. "Where is it? We have a right to that book …"

Given their buttoned-down appearance, the one who stood out was the woman with the buzz cut. She was really big and she was getting loud. She had pushed past Meghan to the archives door and was pulling on the knob.

"Open this door."

"I'm calling security," Meghan said, but the man leaned over and grabbed the phone. Still hiding in the stacks, I pulled out my cellphone.

"Open this door." Now BuzzCut had pulled a pry bar from her jacket. This was getting too weird for me.

I punched 911 and was immediately put on hold. This was not fast enough.

Meghan looked down at the man holding the phone, Mister FiveByFive.

"Would you stop that? Sir?" Meghan stepped closer to him. That didn't strike me as a good idea. "Get away from the phone." He raised his arm to push her away. Then with a loud *crack*, BuzzCut broke the lock on the archives door. Everyone stopped and looked.

I rolled up the copy of the *Necronomicon*, jumped to my feet and headed toward the door. As I passed FiveByFive, I gave him a good whack in the rear end with the book he wanted so much.

"Hey! Losers! You are so hopeless." As I reached the door, I held the book over my head so they could get a good look. Then I waved it at them, the dog-eared pages flapping like owl's wings. "Pissheads! Lookie lookie!"

For a second everyone looked at me. I turned and ran to the top of the stairs; with the new library set-up, the whole area is windows and natural light, and they could still see me from Local History & Archives.

For a few seconds, at the top of the stairs, I felt great. This was like those moments when I have to talk in class, when suddenly, after all the prep and procrastination, the anxiety drains away and I feel brilliant. Here was I now, brilliant. I had surprised everyone. I was in control. I smiled. I waved.

Then I turned, and standing next to me at the top of the stairs was the Proprietor. At the stadium the other night, when he stopped Dana and me, he'd had an amused little smile on his face practically the whole time, this little I'm-so-above-all-of-this smirk. He wasn't smiling now. "Give me the book." He moved between me and the stairs. I wished I was holding a big cup of cold Steely Dan.

"You little…" I felt my magic moment fizzle away. I heard the other two running toward us. The Proprietor grabbed my arm and reached for the *Necronomicon*. I pulled away, and threw the book over the rail.

The book landed on a broad concrete beam. Surprised, the Proprietor loosened his grip. I pulled away from him and vaulted over the rail, following the *Necronomicon*. I balanced on the beam – it was really wide, so it was easy – scooped up the book, jammed it in my backpack and zipped it shut.

I looked back at the second floor of the library. The Proprietor's buddies had joined him. The three of them stood there looking at me.

"Dammit," the Proprietor said. "Move your lazy asses. *I'm* not going after him."

FiveByFive began to climb over the rail. From down the stairs, someone shouted at us. Two security guards had just reached the landing and were coming up the stairs.

"Get back! You!"

I followed the beam to the window, lowered myself over the ledge and dropped. I almost lost my balance when my feet bounced off the rail, but I recovered, hopped onto the landing and scrambled down the stairs to the main floor. I paused and looked back. These people were so stupid.

Then the Proprietor came rocketing down the stairs as fast as I had come, his two buddies right behind him, trailed by the confused security guards. I turned left and ran through both sets of sliding doors, setting off another alarm as I headed into the Jackson Square food court. I sped past the market and the pharmacy's back door, hoping to lose them in the mall – dodging scooters, school kids and old people with walkers – rounded a corner and shot down the stairs to the underground parking lot.

Hamilton's downtown is supposedly depressed and needs reviving, but you wouldn't know it by Jackson Square in the daytime. Up in the mall, it was full of people, and down here in the parking garage, it was full of cars. I don't know if half the people who come through the mall even know the garage exists; I'd never been down there myself, and I didn't figure I'd be followed unless some good citizen in the mall, thinking they were helping catch a thief, pointed me out to the three creeps from the library.

But what do you know, as I hunted between the cars for the York Boulevard exit, who should come clattering down the stairs looking every which way for me?

Uh oh – the exit, which I figured would open onto the street, was blocked by a sliding door. Drivers inserted their paid ticket into a machine to open the exit door to get out. With no ticket, the only way out was to walk back upstairs to the mall – the stairs that BuzzCut, FiveByFive and the Proprietor were coming down right this second. They did not look willing to forgive and forget. I heard an engine starting up and ducked behind a black SUV, until I spotted the car. Sure enough, someone in a beat-up old station wagon was getting ready to go.

"He's down here somewhere," I heard the Proprietor say.

"Why would he come down here? There's no way out."

"'Cause he's too smart for his own good. Search between the cars. You go that way. And you ..."

This was not good. The driver of the station wagon was idling for what seemed like forever. Come on, buddy! – my life is at stake while you scroll through your iPod or, more likely, rummage through your ABBA cassettes.

Now I was getting scared. Once this car pulled out, there would be no witnesses in the parking garage and I was sure that if these three got their hands on me, they would inflict pain and humiliation.

The station wagon was finally moving. The driver backed out, taking it slow in these narrow spaces, and inched toward the exit arrows. I darted from the SUV to the front of a big family van. But it was so big I couldn't see if anyone was coming; I dropped to my knees and scuttled to the next car, another SUV. Bit by bit I was getting closer to the exit.

I wished the station wagon would hurry up and as I listened to the grumble of its engine I worried about suffocating on carbon monoxide. Then I realized that the mall must have a pretty good system to circulate air down here, like those movies where the hero finds a ventilation grill, pries it off with their bare hands and escapes the bad guys through amazingly roomy air ducts. I looked around for such a grill. No such luck.

The station wagon was pulling up to the exit. I wanted to bolt, but if I startled the driver they might just stop what they were doing and roll up their windows. I had to wait. I hugged my backpack to my chest and huddled against the SUV.

When I heard a footstep I turned. BuzzCut was standing two metres behind me, looking the other way. She turned to address the others.

"Are we even sure …?"

As I turned my head to check on the station wagon, BuzzCut saw me and yelled. I crouched there paralyzed; the station wagon driver was just feeding their ticket into the machine. I started to crawl under the SUV but BuzzCut grabbed my ankle. I twisted to break her grip, reached up and grabbed the car's frame, and pulled myself through. I could hear the other two running after me.

Then the sliding door started to rumble. I leaped to my feet, ran past the hissing Proprietor, past the station wagon and rolled under the door just as it cleared the concrete. I kept running up the ramp to the street, dodging traffic as I crossed to the aboveground parking garage on the corner of MacNab.

I had a plan. Up to level 3, then onto the glass-enclosed walkway between the parking garage and Jackson Square; it would be empty this time of day. From there, I could scope out the street three storeys down, and spy on my hopelessly stupid pursuers. If they looked up, I would have lots of time to wave and laugh, and then make my escape.

Out of breath, I punched the button and waited for the elevator. Around the corner I heard a humming and clattering, and a hissing sound that might have been a curse. Oh no, I thought, and around the corner rolled the woman who had stopped me outside the library.

"You have chosen your side," she gasped. "That is good. You have the book. If you keep it …" Hoarse and shuddering, she was a lot more out of breath than I was. For the first time I noticed a transparent tube running up from her clothing and disappearing behind her ear.

"If you let me," she wheezed, "I will …"

I didn't want to "let her" do anything, or even let her anywhere near me. I turned and fled around the corner, hitting the stairs and leaving behind this shambling freak with her odour of garbage and ammonia. I came out on the third floor and warily entered the glass-walled walkway. Below me was the flow of York Boulevard traffic and scattered figures from the men's shelter, zigzagging through the moving cars to the library and Jackson Square. But I couldn't see my three pursuers. Those people, I snickered to myself, they're such losers. Three against one, but here I am. It wasn't even that hard.

From previous visits I knew that at this time of day, an hour could go by without anyone coming through the walkway. I heard the double doors from Jackson Square squeak open, but I was thinking about my next move. I had the *Necronomicon*, but what good was it to me? I liked the idea that the Resurrection Church of the Ancient Gods did *not* have it, since they seemed to think they needed its help to conjure up the Great Old Ones, but what was I going to do with it?

Echoing my thoughts, beside me a voice said, "Just what good is that book … to *you*?" I looked up: the Proprietor was right beside me. I backed away, but bumped into someone on my other side. It was that tall woman, BuzzCut. All three of them were there.

The Proprietor shook his head. "I don't know what it is, but I've got a liking for this boy. I feel like saying … give us the book, my friend, and we'll go our separate ways."

"Give us the book." FiveByFive ripped my backpack off, and I felt BuzzCut gripping my arms. I threw myself forward, grabbed my bag and pushed toward the parking garage. BuzzCut elbowed me in the side of the head and I stumbled, but I didn't let go of the backpack. FiveByFive tugged hard, but I wouldn't move.

"Son, it doesn't have to be like this," the Proprietor said.

"Let go of me." BuzzCut and FiveByFive had now picked me up and, between the two of them, carried me through the doors to the parking garage. Ignoring my struggles, FiveByFive punched the button on the elevator.

"Enough with the stairs," he said. "I'm out of it."

"Let's get him into the van," the Proprietor said. He eyed the numbers over the elevator. It was at 2. "If anyone asks us about him, say 'mall security' and keep going. They'll ignore anything the kid says."

The elevator dinged. There was a pause. I waited for someone to relax their grip, just a bit, and then ...

The doors opened. The scooter lady filled the doorway. She clattered and hummed toward us.

The Proprietor swore. "Back," he said. "Back to the mall."

I was hauled through the doors onto the walkway, but the scooter lady wasn't giving up. Bashing through the doors behind us, she stayed right on our tails.

"This is too far," she wheezed. "You will not without permission beckon Yog-Sothoth. You will not attack the innocent. You will not sacrifice." We stopped in the middle of the walkway and turned to face her. Meanwhile, FiveByFive had been trying to get my backpack away from me, and I had been resisting.

"You little bastard," he hissed. "Let go." He pulled, and even though he was only tugging with one arm, he was too strong for me. I knew I couldn't resist him much longer. He reached into his pocket and pulled something out. With a click, a gleaming blade leapt into his hand.

"Jimmy, put that away," the Proprietor said. "Clare, hold onto him tight." But Jimmy reached forward and slashed at my hands. I tried to recoil, but Clare and Jimmy were too strong. I let go of my backpack, and it was flung to the floor.

"NO!" shouted the woman on the scooter. Suddenly something happened to her; the listless figure on the chair rose up and billowed out and burst forth in the narrow walkway. Clare was thrown to one side, and I was knocked off my feet as something as thick and sinuous as a firehose whipped back and forth through the passage. The Proprietor fled to the doors at the end. From my place on the battered floor of the walkway, I looked up at Jimmy. Something dark and glistening was wrapped around his body – he struggled for breath and looked down at me with bulging, pleading eyes. And another glistening shape like a python was whipping through the air around him, grabbing the knife. And above me was the scooter lady. Her clothes had slipped from her shoulder, showing dark, scaly skin, and the things that held Jimmy and the knife were tentacles. The scooter lady had tentacles.

"*You will raise no weapon*," she hissed, and the dark tentacle stretched like a slingshot – stretched far further than I imagined a living arm could stretch – and hammered the knife so deeply into the ceiling that the glass rattled in the walkway walls. Then it reached down and I felt the arm curl around me and, with infinite softness and strength, glowing from within with a superhuman furnace-like heat, lift me to my feet.

"Proprietor." The woman's tentacles began to withdraw. The Proprietor, heading back toward Jackson Square, stopped in his tracks. The other tentacle dropped Jimmy to the floor; he moaned, but the Proprietor simply stepped over him to approach us.

"You are way out of line here, Interlocutor." The woman, or creature, ignored him, withdrawing one tentacle and using the other to fold and tuck her clothes back into place. In a few moments she appeared, tattered and sick and obese as she seemed, to be a human woman, gesturing with normal arms in billowing clothes and frayed gloves.

"We are going about our business. This is procedure. It's your job to judge and negotiate and liaise, not to intercede. You are supposed to facilitate the coming together of worlds. You can't 'will not' this and 'will not' that. And how dare you attack …"

Wheezing with the effort she had just made, the Interlocutor looked up at him with contempt. "You will not use weapons. Never in my presence."

"Jimmy was just cutting the strap, he didn't hurt him …"

"Uh, actually …" I held up my left hand. It had a slash across the top of it where Jimmy had cut the strap and me both at once. I groped through my pockets for a tissue or an old paper napkin. "Any of you people got a band-aid?"

The Interlocutor ignored me. Whoever or whatever she – or he, or it – was, she was good and mad. "You will not prey on the innocent. When you prey on the innocent, you make victims, and you breed hatred, and you make war. You, Proprietor, you and your people … there are boundaries."

"We are using due process here … and look at this kid … what about him overstepping the boundaries? He just stole an important book from the library, a book that's meant to be a public resource. And he stole it."

"He is no *kid*. He is never a *kid* again!" The Interlocutor spat out the words with contempt. She rolled forward and before I could get out of the way, put her gloved hand, or what passed for a hand, on my shoulder. "You have drawn him into your conspiracies. You dare to raise weapons in my presence. Raise weapons against a young one. Now he is not a child, because you have broken the boundaries. From this moment, I am putting my hand on him."

In fact, I wished she would take her hand off me. As it lay on my shoulder I imagined the pulsing and surging tentacle, grey and lined with tiny black suckers, separated from my skin only by the threadbare fabric of this creature's disguise.

"From this moment," she repeated, "he is under my protection."

Although staying safely out of range, the Proprietor was defiant. He snarled a tough-guy line I remembered from movies: "You don't know who you're messing with."

"Go," said the Interlocutor. She wheezed, and I felt a tremble go through the limb on my shoulder. The tube running up her neck swelled and throbbed. I wondered about her health situation. Perhaps she had an illness – or, it occurred to me, perhaps for such a strange creature, the air we breathed was the wrong kind of air.

"We're outta here. We don't need the book, and we don't need you. You can't protect anyone from anything." The Proprietor turned to go. "You haven't heard the last of me." He and I had obviously watched a lot of the same movies. I waited for him to tell us we'd made ourselves a powerful enemy.

When the Interlocutor had gone into action, Clare had been pushed aside, and wisely had decided to stay aside. Now she got slowly to her feet. I broke away from the Interlocutor and scooped up my backpack. The Proprietor and his henchmen, or henchpersons, headed back toward Jackson Square; Jimmy wistfully looking up at his knife, way out of reach. I looked up at it too – it was stuck into the ceiling so deeply that the entire blade was buried and some of the handle too. The cleaning staff would be scratching their heads over this one.

The Interlocutor turned toward the elevator. After I hooked my backpack over my shoulder on its one good strap, I saw that a swath of her voluminous skirt was torn and dragging behind her. I picked it up and helped her to tuck it in.

"Why do they call you the Interlocutor?"

"They call themselves the followers of Cthulhu – they claim to worship him at their Resurrection Church of the Ancient Gods. When you went to the ceremony, you heard them invoke his name." In her raspy voice, she pronounced *Cthulhu* differently than any I had heard so far. "There are forces who want to build a real ... road ... overpass ..." She waved her gloved hands in the air.

"Bridge?" I suggested.

"Yes, bridge ... bridge, a two-way going. So when there is, someday, a stable continuum threshold, we can have ... relationships, diplomatic relationships. As an Interlocutor it is not for me to take sides. Everyone is to consult me." She shook her bulky head. "But the cult – they are renegades."

The elevator arrived and I held the door while the Interlocutor got in.

The Interlocutor's bizarre aroma filled the elevator and I groped for questions. This thing, or person, was really something else. "What," I asked, "is a continuum threshold?"

The elevator reached the bottom. When the door slid open an old man and his daughter moved to get in, but quickly skittered over to one side to make room for the Interlocutor and me. We passed them and went out into the street. A cold wind blew from the west and suddenly I felt drained and exhausted.

"A bridge between what, and what?" I asked.

"The northern volcanic desert of R'lyhnygoth. But the threshold is weak ..."

"I want to go home," I said.

"Rest," she said. "You will have more to do. However, I must keep moving." The Interlocutor turned to head toward the men's shelter. "I am a renegade too, now.

"Pay close attention to your dreams," she continued. "Cthulhu, if he has awakened, will work through dreams. And as Yog-Sothoth approaches, some will see him in dreams. And if he is allowed to enter this world, there will be no more dreams." She gestured at the buildings and people around us. "All nightmare."

She rolled away down York Boulevard. I walked over to James and while I waited for a bus that would take me home, checked each way to make sure the Proprietor and his friends weren't sneaking up on me. I had my bus pass; sometimes I walk home for the exercise, but I'd spent enough time today being fast on my feet. As I waited I checked my backpack to make sure the *Necronomicon* was still there.

CHAPTER 10
SOMETHING ROCKY

I don't like getting cuts, but I *do* like pouring hydrogen peroxide on cuts and watching it foam up. Science in action. As it foams up, horrible infectious bacteria are having the oxygen stripped away from them until they die. At least that's how I understand it; my dad told me that my mother explained this to him and to me, when I was very young, so it is one of our few bits of shared family lore.

The cut went right across my hand but it wasn't deep. Like the Proprietor had said, Jimmy had only been trying to cut the strap. But you have to be careful with knives. When I was twelve and distributed flyers from my old wagon, I thought a guy had been following me one night, and I told Dad I figured I should carry a knife. I expected him to applaud this as a manly decision, a rite of passage, but instead he swore at me.

"Don't be stupid! If some low-life tries to mess with you, run!"

"But …"

"Knives are for opening envelopes and boxes, and cutting string, and cleaning your nails with. If you want to carry a weapon, join the army." Like I said, I was twelve at the time.

"But …"

"Run. Run home and tell me, or phone the cops." The next time I went out to deliver flyers, he put a sledgehammer in my wagon, "for self-defence." It was so heavy that even with two hands I could barely drag it out and leave it on the lawn. This was the sort of thing Dad considered hilarious.

My next birthday, he gave me a knife with a pinky-sized blade and a host of equally tiny accessories. At Christmas I got a cellphone; a 7-Eleven pay-as-you-go cellphone, but it was my first and I was proud. When I got my first stadium gig, I gave up the flyer delivery job. Considering my financial situation, I often wished I still had it.

After I'd cleaned the cut with peroxide, I painted it with antibiotic ointment, rolled up some gauze and stuck it on with band-aids. Very professional-looking, I thought.

Sweaty from all this running around, I stripped off my jacket and hoodie and poured a glass of iced tea from the jug in the refrigerator. I flopped on the couch and stared at the TV, but didn't turn it on.

Should I have pulled this prank with the *Necronomicon*? It had only gotten me more tangled up with these creepy Resurrection Church people. I didn't like them one bit and I could tell the feeling was mutual.

Then again, *the scooter lady had tentacles.* She was definitely not from around here. There had to be other worlds involved, worlds I'd never heard of, other races, other species. None of the movies in the science fiction section at Touchdown Video (all of it now in boxes or on shelves all over our house), none of the books I'd ever read included anything quite like the Interlocutor.

I pulled the *Necronomicon* out of my backpack and looked through it. Spells, some of them in a language that looked like Latin, some translated into English. At the beginning of the book was a two-line epigraph:

That is not dead which can eternal lie,
And with strange aeons even death may die.

I wrinkled my nose. Yuck. Was *this* what I was risking my life for, my freedom, my valuable rear end? Some rotten poetry? If that wasn't bad enough, the book seemed to be linked with some kind of death-worshipping or devil-worshipping cult that, lame as its ideas might be, seemed to be capable of impossible stunts like conjuring storm clouds and summoning huge centipede-type monsters into a football stadium. A cult led by some plastic-looking white guy who was annoyingly self-assured and commanded muscular thugs. Plus, the scooter lady had tentacles. Thank god none of these people, or things, knew my name or where I lived.

There was a knock on the front door.

The venetian blinds over the living-room window were closed and I peeked out. A cab pulled away from in front of the house. There was some middle-aged dude on the porch; thin brown hair high up on his pale forehead, wide-set eyes and a pinched, worried-looking mouth. He was wearing an old-fashioned looking suit, and a shirt and tie like a motivational speaker or a school principal.

No way I was answering the door. This guy had Resurrection Church written all over him. I know we shouldn't go by appearances, but if I opened the door I would get sucked back into this scary and screwed up new world I'd stumbled into when I snuck into the stadium. I peeked again. This guy looked like he was an expert on screwy old books, spoke dead languages better than he spoke English and thought human sacrifice was okay if agreed to by a show of hands.

The Resurrection Church had found me after all. I worried that when Dad got back from work, they would find him too – but it was me they wanted. I needed to get away.

As soon as the man in the suit gave up and turned away from our front door, I rushed upstairs and emptied out my backpack. Then I refilled it with stuff I figured I would absolutely need: laptop, flashlight, matches, toothbrush, et cetera. This was the emergency stash I kept in my dresser. If school, home and Hamilton ever got too much for me, I had intended to amass enough spare change to, if necessary, buy a bus ticket to someplace far away and exotic, or at least on the fringes of civilization: San Francisco, Guadalajara, Whitehorse. I counted my stash: six toonies. Well, twelve bucks is better than nothing. Downstairs, I filled a bottle with water, threw some granola bars into the backpack's side pocket and put on my hoodie and jacket.

I peeked through the blinds again. The man on the porch was now out on the sidewalk. He looked up and down the street; he looked at our house; he looked at his wristwatch; then, producing a cellphone that he stared at as if some hideous parasite had attached itself to his hand, he started gingerly keying in a number.

My phone started to ring. Was this a coincidence, or did this guy have my number? I was tempted to answer it and ask what was up. But then I thought of the goons at the library and the crowd of people in front of the stadium the other night. How many people were tied up with the Resurrection Church? Once this guy knew I was in the house, he might show up on my porch with an army. I sat still, feeling trapped and peeking outside from time to time until, looking exasperated, the man in the suit headed down the street and was gone.

I made sure the front door was locked, headed through the kitchen and slipped out the back door, locking it behind me. Our back yard was empty. At the far end, through the screen of bamboo fronds, I could see Rocky's hopeful black face poking through the chain-link fence. I suppressed a quick impulse to go back in the house for some marrow bones, and headed up the narrow lane between our house and the neighbour's.

I came around the corner of our porch to see an enormous black SUV coming down the street, the kind of car my dad always says sarcastic things about.

"Here we are, running out of fossil fuels," Dad likes to point out, "and the cars are getting bigger and bigger."

Personally, I hated cars – maybe because I blamed them for killing my mother, I don't really know – so I am no expert on the subject, but eventually I saw what he meant. Walking through downtown as night fell, lately I was seeing more and more of these enormous vehicles. Dodge Rams cruising James Street on Friday nights; Ridgelines big enough for six, a solitary driver slowing to check out the teenage girls on their way to weekend parties; or any one of those destroyer-like SUVs, their model names jumbled images of nature and conquest – Expedition,

Terrain, Sequoia, Armada, Yukon – as if their sole purpose was to speed their drivers away to wilderness strongholds in the advent of an apocalypse.

But for all that, I might not have paid any attention to the huge black Escalade that pulled up across the street from my house, if the door hadn't opened and Kara, the girl from the stadium, hadn't climbed out of it. She spoke to someone inside, pointed at my house, smiled and started down the street, swinging her school backpack over her shoulder – she lived just a few streets away.

Kara, jeez. We'd had our differences years ago – in grade five she got me called to the principal's office by telling the teacher that I'd had a knife in my backpack – but now we were older and I thought we'd put that behind us. We got along okay when we worked the stadium concessions at football games. I felt betrayed.

As the Escalade idled in the street, BuzzCut and FiveByFive – oops, I mean Clare and Jimmy – emerged. I headed out to the sidewalk to run down the street, but coming up from the corner was the geeky-looking guy in the suit. He spotted me, broke into a hopeful smile and raised his hand.

I headed back down the narrow laneway between our house and the neighbour's, but Jimmy, moving with unexpected speed, was already on the porch beside me. He lunged down to grab my backpack but I was too fast. Jimmy came over the rail and hit the ground behind me, and I charged through our gate and across our backyard, then leapt through the bamboo leaves, hooking my legs over the half-concealed chain-link fence. The bamboo scrabbled at my pack, and I had to tug the cut strap off a snag, then I was into Melanie's yard and Rocky was leaping up, trying to lick my face.

"Attaboy," I said, one hand petting that big froggy head as I crossed the yard, the other hand reaching out to hit the gate latch. In a second I was tugging at the unfamiliar hardware and opening the gate. I leaned down and gave Rocky one last scratch behind the ears.

"See ya later, bud." I heard the sound of a body crashing through the leaves and over the fence behind us. Then I was through the gate, latching it behind me as Rocky snarled and rushed to meet the intruder. "That's my Rocky," I said to myself, as a howl of pain came from Jimmy. Then I was out in the street and running east toward the stadium.

"Help," I heard a frightened voice call out behind me. "No! Getoffa me! Help!" For a moment I felt sorry for Jimmy. Dork he may be, but this wasn't really his fault. He just hadn't put in the time making friends with Rocky.

CHAPTER 11
SOMEONE EXILED

With Jimmy hollering behind me, I ran out onto Rosemont and up Barnesdale. Stopping to catch my breath, I saw the Escalade nose around the corner, so I ducked into the lane that ran behind the storefronts to Lottridge, ran through the Big Bee parking lot, then crossed Barton to the Tim Hortons. From inside, I could see the street better than anyone outside could see me.

I bought some Timbits and ate one or two while I waited. No one came looking for me. Keeping off the street as much as I could, I cut through the car wash and the FreshCo parking lot and headed down Gage, turning east on Primrose to pass the abandoned textile factory. Before I got to Belview Park, I came to a rundown-looking duplex, its sagging porch freshly painted blue and white. This was Sam's house.

I knocked on the door. Through its window I could see Sam's sister Mehri; she saw me and called to her brother. I waved to her and tried the door. It was locked, but Mehri unlatched it and let me in.

"Oh boy," she said, "Timbits."

Mehri smiled and her face kind of lit up. I tried to smile back, but just made a pathetic whimpering sound and coughed to clear my throat. Mehri has big dark eyes and when she smiles her face, framed by soft black hair, seems to open up and … the overall effect is hard to describe. She has a gracefully arched nose – *aquiline* I would call it, having learned that word from the novel *Dracula*, where Dracula is described as having an aquiline nose. How is this relevant? Well, it makes him distinguished-looking, and he is also (you know this if you've read *Dracula*) from the East – as was Mehri, but I shouldn't go on and on about this, because at this point the connections start to get fuzzy. Once, in a rare moment alone with Mehri, trying to be hip and urbane, I tried to explain them to her – Dracula, the East, aquilinity – and, well, it had just ended in an uncomfortable silence.

Anyway, just about anything Mehri does with her face seems very profound to me. Sometimes I have to look away.

"So, Nate, do you want to come in?"

"Sure," I said. "I mean, yes, thanks, of course." Since the Dracula conversation, Mehri looks at me with this little smile, like she's waiting for the next hilarious goofy thing her brother's Anglo friend is going to say. Sam clattered down the stairs.

"Nate. Timbits. Awesome."

"Everybody seems to like them," I said weakly.

"I'm just making supper, Nate," Sam's mother said. "Would you like to have some rice with us?"

"Uhh, actually, Mrs. Shirazi … I dunno…" Actually, I was so hungry I was afraid I'd eat everything. As usual, Sam's mother insisted. "Some rice" turned out to be a spiced chicken stew thingy called *khoresh*, which we scooped up with a flatbread that I already knew as *lavash*.

Sam and I had gotten to know each other in grade eight when we were paired up for a class project. He and his family were new to the country and Sam's English was minimal. I began to help him out after class. I didn't have many friends myself, and my father and I did not make up much of a family, but it was hard to feel sorry for myself when I saw the Shirazis, fresh from Iran and starting from scratch in everything they did, from saying good morning in English to finding jobs.

"I am a master of many skills," Mr. Shirazi had said to me once. "Writer and newspaper reporter, I can run a variety of web- and sheet-fed offset printing presses, and I can service PCs and I have a master's degree in Persian literature from the University of Tehran. But at the moment, I am driving a taxicab."

Sam turned out to be smart and motivated, and he helped me feel smart and motivated too. Being new to everything in

Hamilton, Sam was something of an outsider, and I tended to be a loner also. Maybe it was too many days at the library looking up books on dinosaurs and science and astronomy (lately also art, ancient and modern, especially drawing), film, Charles Dickens, you name it ... too many black-and-white Universal horror movies, I don't know. Anyway, I had spent a lot of time at his house, and I was thinking I might ask to stay the night.

Before we did the dishes, I checked the time and phoned Dad. He was home from work and asked me what the hell was going on.

"There's some guys in a big black SUV; I swear to god they're staking the place out. I went and knocked on their window and they told me they were waiting for a buddy. I asked 'em who their buddy was and said I was calling the cops and they just laughed. It was kind of a beefy-looking guy and a woman – real big lady with a sort of rakish haircut."

"Dad, watch out for those people." I was parroting back exactly what he had said to me last night.

"I called the cops on 'em. But that was an hour ago and no one's shown up."

"Don't let them in the house."

"Of course not. Nate – where are you and what are you doing?" He was relieved to hear that I was at the Shirazis.

"Sam and I are working on an essay for school ..."

"On a Saturday night?"

"I'm getting my butt in gear, like you always tell me I should. I'm going to stay over."

Dad didn't complain. "That's what you need," he said. "People around you. A real family. Give me a call in the morning."

Chances are I could have stayed. But for some reason I didn't even ask. Since the night at the stadium, I was starting to feel more and more like some kind of creep magnet. Who knows, if this Yog-Sothoth/Cthulhu/Old Ones stuff was true, maybe the Resurrection Church was homing in on me through some kind of paranormal force; eventually it would come round to the Shirazis too. That was the last thing this family needed; Sam had told me a little bit about what they had been through before they left Iran.

Then I figured out the perfect place to spend the night, where no one would find me. Genius, pure genius.

A nineties-vintage Toyota RAV4 pulled into the driveway and Sam's dad came out along with his oldest sister, Hamideh. I greeted them and said I had to go, but before I left, I pulled out the *Necronomicon*. "Mr. Shirazi," I asked, "have you ever heard of this thing?"

Sam's mother looked over my shoulder at the book and dismissed it with a wave of her hand. "This is just another Westerner writing down their silly ideas about the East."

Mr. Shirazi nodded. "This is a Western invention, Nate. The *Necronomicon*. Some European, or Euro-American type like Lovecraft, writing down his fantasies and passing it off as folklore. Just like the *Arabian Nights*."

"So, you *have* heard of it."

"It's insulting," Mrs. Shirazi said.

"I'm sorry, it's not that I believe any of it, but I've got kind of a problem," I said. "Lately I've run into people who seem to take this book very seriously."

"Spells and devil worship – this is fairy tale," said Mrs. Shirazi.

"Nate," said Mr. Shirazi, "don't buy into this kind of prejudice. You think because we're Persian we'll know all about this? 'The Mad Arab.' That's just because we're from what everyone here calls the Middle East…"

"Sorry, Mr. Shirazi. I'm asking everyone I meet, because…"

"Lovecraft was a typical North American xenophobe who was afraid of everything and everybody that didn't come from white America or northern Europe. He was a fantasy writer who made up everything he wrote, based on old books by English and northern European writers, who were also xenophobes and imperialists and racists and who made up stories and called them Asian culture …"

"Mr. Shirazi, I'm sure that's true, but I'll tell you, lately there've been some very strange things …"

"Besides," Mr. Shirazi harrumphed, "Not only was he not Persian, he wasn't even an Arab. Everybody knows that Abdul Alhazred was a goddamned Egyptian."

CHAPTER 12
SOMETHING IN THE DARK

As I walked back through Belview Park, I felt my cellphone vibrate. I sat on a bench and read this text message:

Hope all is well. Could we meet @ Homegrown Hamilton café on King William St., 11 am tomorrow? Mutual co-operation can only be beneficial! <HPL>

Well, I didn't know anyone else at the Hamilton Public Library, so HPL must be that librarian, Meghan. "Hope all is well." Did this mean she was thinking about me, even worried about my well-being? She should be. Even though she'd been snarky and officious, I'd decoyed – heroically decoyed, I might add – the Resurrection Church creeps away from her and made off with a book she claimed to hate. I texted back, *See you there.*

TONIGHT, HOWEVER, to make sure that the Resurrection Church stayed away from me and anyone I cared about, I decided to go where no one would find me: I would surprise Dana and spend the night sharing his luxury squat at Prince of Wales Elementary. After all, I had overnight gear, a bottle of water and granola bars I was willing to share. What else could I need?

It was just after nine, and the sun was down. When I reached PoW I found my flashlight and slipped it into my pocket. Across the street, the empty stadium slept, and the neighbourhood was dead quiet. I looked around, but saw no one as I approached the ground-floor window. The plywood rattled when I touched it; if it was loose, that meant Dana must be inside. Sure enough, when I poked at it, I saw that it was on the hook.

"Dana," I called quietly through the crack. "Dana! It's me."

I listened; there was no response except for a far-off hiss, like oil sputtering in a frying pan. Probably one of PoW's noisy old steam radiators. "Dana!" I called, watching the street for passersby.

Well, if he was so far inside he couldn't hear me and come let me in, this plan could go up in smoke. I tugged on the plywood but it wouldn't open more than a few centimetres. I tried my pocket knife, but its tiny blade wouldn't reach the hook. But there's always junk around construction sites; I groped around on the ground, and in a few seconds found a thin splinter of wood. I stuck it through the crack and popped the hook on Dana's makeshift latch. Then I pulled back the plywood sheet and slipped through.

I recognized this room. As I remembered, it had been an empty classroom, used to store old blackboards and wooden desks; now it was stripped down to cracked cement walls and, in the ceiling, gaping sockets where they had ripped out the fluorescent lights. "Dana, it's me!" I called in a loud whisper.

What was that smell? It turned my stomach like something rotten, but it was sharper than, say, a dead animal. Gas, I thought, maybe that hissing sound was gas. I wrinkled my nose and breathed through my mouth. If there was a natural gas leak and Dana was inside – and I was sure that if he'd left, he would have screwed shut his secret entrance – he could be passed out in here somewhere; could even die, if I didn't get to him fast.

From down the hall came a prolonged hiss that built to a hoarse rattle, *Ashshhhchikkachikkachikka* ... I pushed the plywood sheet back onto the hook and groped for the door, then rounded the corner into the hall where, now that I was away from the window, I dared to turn on my flashlight. In its harsh beam, the air churned with blue smoke, and the smell was stronger than ever. But smoke would mean fire, and if there was a fire, I wouldn't be smelling gas: the whole place would have gone up and there would be flames and black smoke and the smell of burning plaster, wood and wiring.

So there was no danger from fire. Somehow, realizing this didn't make me feel safer.

From the end of the hall, toward the gymnasium, I heard the sound again, *Ashshhhchikkachikkachikka*, and I thought, sure enough, this is a gas leak and that sound – was it the sound of someone injured, or suffocating? "Dana!" I called and rushed toward the gym, but suddenly I was gripped by nausea; the floor seemed to spin and I sank to my knees. The flashlight skittered across the dusty floor. Dizzy, I crawled toward it, noticing in the dust the criss-crossed treads of many workboots. Ahead of me came that sound again. Suddenly the building shuddered. My ears popped, like a change in air pressure before a big storm. A waft of cold air, laden with that awful stink, blew from the gym's open doors. The beam of my flashlight dimmed and went out – and then came back again as bright as before. My head began to clear. If this was no gas leak, I thought, then what was it? I wanted to bolt back through the window and run and not come back. But I thought of Dana, somewhere there in the dark – and of how gas rises, doesn't it? – so just in case, I'd stay down on the floor, hoping that gave me a better chance of getting through this. I picked up my flashlight and crawled toward the gym.

The doors were ajar. Sure enough, as soon as I got inside I rotated the light and saw that I had found Dana's nighttime nest. Through the plumes of bluish smoke I saw a few household items: a bottle of water, a jar of peanut butter and a can of silver spray paint. Amid the workmen's boot prints on the dusty floor, I saw other marks – the prints of enormous three-toed paws. If someone had brought a dog in here, it must have been a huge one. The prints were everywhere.

Then, like discarded slippers, the pale soles of Dana's bare feet, dead centre in the floor. I called his name again, and sniffed. The awful stink was still there, but it was fading, and the old school building had gone eerily silent. Whatever I'd heard, it had gone away, far away. Dana didn't move. I stood up, sniffed the air again and walked toward him.

DAVID NEIL LEE

"Dana?"

The smoke was clearing, and around Dana were scattered flakes of ashes and charred clothing. For sure they were Dana's clothes, because Dana himself was naked; his pale, bony body lay squarely in the centre of the coloured lines on the dusty gym floor. There was some kind of gunk, something bluish smeared all over him, and his eyes were wide open on his battered face. Worse yet, that battered face was no longer on top of his neck where it belonged, but was sitting on Dana's chest, where his severed head was carefully arranged between his dead hands.

PART 2
THE HOUNDS

"No words in our language can describe them!"
[Chalmers] spoke in a harsh whisper. "They are
symbolized vaguely in the myth of the Fall, and in
an obscene form which is occasionally found
engraved on the ancient tablets. The Greeks had a
name for them, which veiled their essential foulness.
The tree, the snake and the apple – these are the
vague symbols of a most awful mystery."
– Frank Belknap Long, *The Hounds of Tindalos*

CHAPTER 13
ENEMIES OF THE CHURCH

I woke up with a great upsetting lurch, my resting place quaking under me.

"What the hell is this?" A man's outraged voice.

"Oh... hey..."

I forced my eyes open, surprised that some dude was yelling at me, but even more surprised that I had fallen asleep. It had taken me hours ... hours while I mourned that Dana was gone, hours while I fretted that whatever had gotten him now had my scent and was shuffling through the shadows, hissing and chittering, getting closer and closer. But I'd felt that here, I was in a safe place... if only I could doze off, just for an hour, I'd be up and out of there before anyone found me. For hours, listening and waiting and reliving what I'd seen in the abandoned school, I tossed and turned in the dark, but once I fell asleep, I crashed like a skid full of bricks.

"What do you think you're doing in my car?"

"Sorry, Mr. Shirazi." I pushed myself up off the back seat. "I thought I'd be outta here before anybody got up. I was kind of uh, on the run last night." Outside the old Toyota, it was just getting light. I didn't think anyone would be up this early on a Sunday morning – not even Sam's dad.

"Get out!" He opened the passenger door to let me out of the back seat where I'd spent the night. He slammed the door as I stood there, still wobbly from sleep.

"What do you mean by 'on the run'?"

"It's hard to ..."

"Are you on drugs? Because if you are, you must stay away from Osama. Stay away from my family." He leaned down and looked me in the eyes. "I thought you were too smart for that, Nate."

"Jeez, Mr. Shirazi ... it's not like that. Weird things have been happening in this part of town. I've been trying to find out about this Church ..." I cleared my throat.

My voice was hoarse from rehearsing a growly voice, trying to disguise it in the 911 call I made from the Big Bee pay phone a few hours before.

Sam's dad looked skeptical and I couldn't blame him. I talked fast. "... and the next thing I know, these people – I think they killed my mother, years ago. And now they've come back."

"Not the Resurrection Church of the Ancient Gods."

"I think they're after ... Hey, how did you know?"

"Get back in the car." Mr. Shirazi looked around anxiously at the fading shadows. He got in and started up the engine.

After I had found Dana's body, I got out of PoW and ran. But it was late, I was cold and I had no place else to go. Still afraid to go home, I'd thought I would sneak into the Shirazis' car – I knew the driver's door didn't lock properly – and spend the night on the back seat (I didn't think it would be so uncomfortable; I'd forgotten that cars have seat belts). Then I'd get up and leave in the morning before anyone could discover me.

Some plan. Mr. Shirazi backed out of the driveway and we started toward my house through the network of narrow streets, quiet at this time of the morning. He shook his head.

"Mrs. Shirazi and I tried to be casual when you showed up at our house with that ... book ... but it made us both worried. I mean, you are a young man, still just a boy really, and it's your right to be young and stupid, but getting mixed up with the Resurrection Church of the Ancient Gods and going around town flashing a copy of the *Necronomicon*, that's as bad as getting mixed up with drugs."

At the Melrose Avenue stop sign we could see the front of PoW, swarming with the strobing lights of an ambulance and a pack of patrol cars; the sidewalk was marked off with police tape.

"Something is going on at the school." Mr. Shirazi pulled into the intersection and idled, trying to get a better look.

"Keep going!" I burst out. "You don't wanna know what went down there!"

"I'm sure you're right." He looked at me curiously and accelerated, continuing west.

"A guy got killed there," I said. "It's got something to do with the Church."

"How do you know that?"

Mr. Shirazi was asking me something. Before he started preaching to me again, I thought I should seize the moment.

"Because I keep finding out stuff I don't want to know. I'm not mixed up with the Church. I'd like to just ignore them and hope they go away. But a few nights ago, a friend of mine and I snuck into one of those midnight games, those rituals. We saw some ... stuff that looked impossible. I researched some stuff online, and went to the library to look at the *Necronomicon*. Well, one thing sort of led to another and I ended up running off with the library's copy of it. And ...." How should I describe the person, or thing, or creature called the Interlocutor? "... in doing that, I found out some more ... really weird stuff. And now the people in the Church are after me. They followed me to my house."

"And then what happened? More 'stuff'?"

I was silent. At this point, if Mr. Shirazi had been *my* father, I would tell him to shove it, he would get mad and later we would both apologize and have a laugh. But he wasn't my father.

"Mr. Shirazi," I said. "Let me out of the car, please."

He raised his eyebrows, but kept driving. "Why? I'm taking you home."

"Because for all I know, you're a member of the Church."

"What?" The car lurched to the side as he pulled over at the corner of Lottridge. "How dare you say that to me."

"I told you the Church is staking out my house. And you're taking me to my house."

"I demand an apology."

"You're going on about how young and stupid I am and I'm sure you're right, but that's the same way the Proprietor talks to me." Mr. Shirazi stared straight ahead, his hands on the wheel, and huffed. We sat there in an angry silence.

I continued, "The Proprietor is the head of the Resurrection ..."

"I know who the Proprietor is. His name is Raphe Therpens. For years he was a lawyer, out west, working for the oil industry. Until he found something bigger."

I felt for the door handle. If Mr. Shirazi was part of this too, what did it mean for Sam and his sisters? What did it mean for Mehri? Did I have to warn them about their own father?

In the angled glow of the street lights Mr. Shirazi took a deep breath. He sat there and looked at me. "Nate, it's true that I know more than you think about the Resurrection Church of the Ancient Gods. But don't ever believe that I might join them, or that I approve of them, or that I can even coexist with them, any more than they can tolerate me You may think that they're small and local, but don't be fooled. The Church is huge. And it is everywhere. I won't talk to you now about our reasons for leaving Iran and coming here. It is too personal, and for you it may be dangerous to know. But let me tell you how disappointed I was when we came to Canada, and settled down, and started to build new lives, and then found that the Church was here too.

"This so-called church, this cult," he continued, "they prey on people new to the country, people who are frightened and vulnerable. They tell them there's a better way to get ahead, by worshipping these twin gods, Cthulhu and Yog-Sothoth, and their nest of aliens, the Great Old Ones who are trying to break through to this world. Wherever they go, they target the helpless, and attack those who would try to do good. They prey on people who are poor, and frustrated, and alone, and who have lost hope. I know ..." He looked over at the dark bulk of the stadium, silent as the grey dawn light of crept through the sleeping neighbourhood.

"Totally," I said. "The Church are a bunch of fricking Nazis." I was starting to feel a flicker of hope.

"I still wonder sometimes," he said. "I wonder if I've brought my family to the right place, or whether if we'd stayed home, if somehow ..."

I was finding Sam's dad hard to read at this point.

Then he shook his head and said, "But that's not here or there. What kind of forces have the Church put around your house? How many?"

"It was just a car with two people when I talked to my dad. But that was hours ago. Now, there might not be anybody."

"We'll drive by your house, and if we see a vehicle keeping your place under surveillance, I will make a call. In ten minutes, I can have a dozen men here. Then we will convince the Church people to leave."

"There was just one vehicle. A big black SUV."

Mr. Shirazi smiled. "If they're watching for you and waiting to pounce, they'll be very sorry."

"Mr. Shirazi, you have no idea what these people are like."

We turned down Somerset, and pulled up in front of my house. It was dark. The street was quiet. Everything looked normal. I got out and looked around. The Escalade was gone.

"Yes, I do," Mr. Shirazi said. He turned off the car. As we walked to the porch he felt through his pockets and handed me a card. "We can help you. Call me."

"Thanks." I pocketed the card without looking at it, and unlocked the front door. Mr. Shirazi looked both ways down the quiet street before coming inside with me.

I turned on the front hall light; the main floor was empty, everything looked in order. Dad's old hollow-body Gibson guitar leaned against the couch: Dad had been up late. Still, I felt a flood of relief. It had been a long night.

"Don't spend nights outside, Nate. Keep your phone charged. Call if you need help."

"Sorry about using your car. I was going to stay somewhere else. But it didn't work out."

I almost told him about my visit to Dana, about how I'd found Dana, about what had happened. I was dying to tell somebody. But I had the feeling that the more people knew about my situation, the worse it would get. (I have since learned that it's usually the other way around.)

Then he left. As the door closed I heard a voice from upstairs.

"Is that you?" My father called.

"Yes. It's me."

Dad appeared at the top of the stairs in his dressing gown. He stretched lazily, acting as if he'd just got up from a delicious snooze, but he looked awful, haggard and anxious.

"I was a bit worried," he yawned. "Even though I knew you were safe with Sam and his family."

"What about those guys who were watching the house?"

"They took off when Melanie showed up. She was onto one of them about staying the hell out of her yard. She was more than usually irate. She also told me to tell you to stay out of their yard. I didn't understand everything she said. Someone got bit by Rocky? Not you, I hope."

Dad came downstairs and sat in the old armchair at the end of the couch.

"It's the Resurrection Church thing," I said. "One of those creeps chased me, so I did what you always told me to do. Ran like hell."

"I thought we had an agreement that we would leave those people alone."

"I was in the wrong place at the wrong time." I told him that after a normal sleepover at Sam's house, Mr. Shirazi had given me a ride home.

"At six o'clock on a Sunday morning?" Dad proceeded to point out the holes in my story. He lectured me on how dangerous the Church could be, but also how, since they were so single-minded, they could easily be avoided. He reminded me how, stern as he might sound at the moment, he was always there for me. Or at least, this is what, later in the morning, he told me he'd said, because after talking to me for several minutes, he realized I'd fallen asleep on the couch, and was not benefitting from his wisdom.

Lying there on my back, I dreamt of blood and blue smoke, and Dana lying on the dusty floor with his severed head between his pale hands, and of something monstrous that had come out of the night and, having finished its work with Dana, greeted me with parched chittering sounds in the dark, and left behind only death, and smears of goo, and monstrous three-toed footprints.

I woke up when I heard Dad getting ready to go to work, and looked at my phone. *Meghan. Homegrown. 11 am.* I took a shower and changed my clothes. I picked up the library copy of the *Necronomicon*. Did I need it? No. Did the Resurrection Church want it? Yes. Couldn't I make life easier for myself by going to their headquarters and dropping it off?

No. To hell with those people.

I searched my bookshelves. No way, if they managed to jump me, was I sacrificing *Planet Hulk, Aliens vs. Predator Omnibus* or *Gustave Doré: Life and Art.* I looked through the books my mother had left that no one had looked at in ten years. I found a title, wrapped it in some pages from the *Spectator*, wrote *Necromonicon* on one side of it in magic marker and looked at it for a minute. Did I spell that right? On the other side, for good measure, I wrote *Necronomicon.* It was all just confusing. Dad was heading out the door, so I stuck the book in a shopping bag and took the bus downtown with him, leaving him to change buses at MacNab as I headed to the café.

CHAPTER 14
HPL

Scanning the downtown streets, I saw no signs of Mister-perfect-hair Proprietor, or Clare and Jimmy. And after all, unless they'd shadowed me, why should they be there? They had their own church, out among the weeds and train tracks at the end of Markle Avenue. In the corner of a parking lot I saw the familiar logo, as always with a different slogan:

NEW JERUSALEM

BUILDED HERE!

There was nothing scary about that; the logo was everywhere these days.

On Homegrown's patio, a skinny, grey-haired woman in a print dress smoked a cigarette with one hand and held her wool coat closed against the autumn wind with the other. She ignored me, but I kept my eye on her as I approached. When I saw her take a last puff and shiver, I shivered too. For all I knew she was a cult member watching me as warily as I was watching her. I thought of turning around and going home. But where would that get me? In her text message, Meghan had said, "mutual co-operation can only be beneficial." She hadn't been to a midnight game, or seen what happened to Dana, but after our dustup at the library maybe she was starting to take the Resurrection Church of the Ancient Gods more seriously. I stepped inside and scanned the few customers the place had this Sunday morning. Meghan wasn't one of them.

Some kind of folksy music was playing in the background and there was a warm aroma of coffee and baked goods, so I immediately craved muffins. I sat down a little ways from the door and pulled out my phone. I looked at it intently. Not because I had an urgent message – as usual, there was nothing – but because I wanted to look busy and distracted, since, like an idiot, I hadn't grabbed anything to eat at home, and now I was starving.

Besides, if I was going to spend any time in the café, I would have to buy something. I figured that the change left over from buying yesterday's Timbits should be plenty, but I furtively checked the menu over the bar to see what was cheapest.

Muffin. Hot chocolate. That should do it. Where was that change? I groped through my jacket pockets, then my hoodie pockets, then my pants pockets. There was a draft of cold air as someone entered the café.

"Excuse me – might you be Nathan Silva?"

Where the hell was my money? Finally I found it. Not as much as I'd figured. Then I looked up.

Looking down at me was not Meghan, but the weird-looking dude who had come to my house the day before. With his tweedy suit jacket, white shirt and wisp of dark hair over his pale forehead, he looked like he had been photoshopped into the café from *It's a Wonderful Life* (bank teller) or the *Godfather* trilogy (frightened bystander). I suddenly forgot how hungry I was and panicked. I looked around for others, but this guy had come alone.

"Sorry." He had extended his hand to shake mine, but I didn't know what to do. Finally he gave up and sat down across from me. "I didn't mean to scare you."

I tried not to look as nervous as I felt. Still, at least he was acting friendly. No one in the Church had ever done that to me.

I looked around. It was Sunday morning and not very busy, but everyone else seemed to be minding their own business. This didn't seem like an ambush. The guy's tone was amiable and at just this moment, the emptiness of my pockets had given me a sinking feeling. I needed someone who would buy me breakfast.

I blurted out, "But where's Meghan?"

He looked at his wristwatch. "Of course, the young woman from the library. I certainly hope she makes it. She wasn't sure she could. I tried to impress upon her the urgency of our problems. One of our members told me that the library's copy of the '71 *Necronomicon* went missing on her shift." He shook his head. "So difficult to convince the average person just how dire the situation is. That's why I'm so glad you responded to my text."

"What text was that?"

He looked puzzled. "I texted you that we should meet here; surely that's why you came."

"But it was Meghan who texted me."

I pulled out my phone and checked Messages. Who else would it come from? The signature was HPL – and she was the only person I'd met at the Hamilton Public Library.

I looked up and saw Meghan out on the sidewalk. She was wrapped in a black overcoat and a long turquoise scarf. As she closed the door behind her and swept into the café, everyone looked. I half-stood to make sure she saw me, at the same time wincing as I recalled how cold and snarky she'd been at the library.

"I've got less than an hour," Meghan said by way of greeting. She unbuttoned her coat and sat down.

"Did you send me a text?" I asked. She shook her head.

"Actually, it's rather funny," said the man in the suit. He smiled. "The text was from me. Let me introduce myself, please." He extended his hand again. "H. P. Lovecraft."

"Sure," I rolled my eyes and finally shook hands; his was big and bony and shook mine firmly. "And I'm Charles Dickens," I said.

"Lovecraft" smiled. "It's a long and complicated story," he said. "Much longer and more complicated than anything I ever wrote. And please, call me Howard."

Now I knew why he'd struck me as familiar when I'd first sighted him on my front porch. I had looked up Lovecraft online only the day before. A skinny white guy from one of the New England states, with a long, pale face that didn't quite fit together: his wide-set dark eyes had a warm and humorous look, but his thin lips, tightly pursed in his long narrow jaw, gave his lower face an anxious expression.

"This is hilarious," I said. Another thing I knew, or had a vague impression, about H. P. Lovecraft was that he had died a long time ago.

The server came over and let us know if we wanted anything we had to order at the counter. "Of course." The man in the suit looked at me. "Can I treat you to something, Nathan?"

"You sure can. Hot chocolate, and maybe a muffin, please?" I began to warm up to this guy a little. He went up to the bar.

I looked at Meghan, then at the bar where "HPL" was chatting with the server. Meghan looked at me.

"H. P. Lovecraft?"

She rolled her eyes. "Be nice. I know he's quirky and has a face like an ant. But he came to see me at the library and I find him weirdly gauche and charming."

"If you didn't text me, why are you here?"

"After you put on your show at the library yesterday, Howard showed up. By the way ... just what was that all about? You weren't very nice to your Resurrection Church buddies."

"They're not my buddies. In fact, every time we meet, we hate each other just a little bit more."

"If that's the case, they're probably not someone you should prank."

"I wasn't pranking them," I sighed. "I was leading them away from you so nobody would get hurt."

"Oh. I never thought of that." For a moment Meghan was speechless. "Well, thanks."

"Also because I wanted to annoy them. So why are you here?"

"Howard said he was in town to find out what the Church is

up to. So I guess you know all about this group, the Lovecraft Underground?"

"I emailed them once."

She chuckled. "If everyone in the Underground is like Howard, it must be a real geekfest. LUG, give me a break!"

"Well, this Lovecraft guy seems a lot nicer than the Proprietor and his goons." I smiled politely, secretly hoping that LUG had more firepower than she gave them credit for.

"The League of Unmarried Gentlemen," she chuckled. "But Howard says you're the one who alerted them to the latest activities of the Resurrection Church of the Ancient Gods. He also says that we have to act right away to avert a disaster of cosmic, earth-changing proportions. I'm not so sure about that, but I have some serious questions about this Resurrection Church – especially after yesterday. Dealing with people like that isn't in my job description." She rolled her eyes. "I'm going to get a latte."

We joined the alleged Mr. Lovecraft, and as we waited for Meghan's coffee I sipped the hot chocolate that Lovecraft had bought me and was handed a carrot muffin.

"Nate, here, was a big hit at the library the other day," Meghan said.

"Oh yes," said Lovecraft distractedly. He was looking out the café window, where a group of young people – the guys in baseball caps, the girls in hoodies – rambled past, pushing each other and laughing.

"I just wanted to look at the *Necronomicon*."

"I know," she replied. "I've been told to call the cops immediately if those people show up again. You are not exactly welcome either; I wouldn't come back soon if I were you. I explained to the security guards that those guys were chasing you. But they weren't very happy about you jumping out onto the beams like that."

"I was going to get my butt kicked!"

"There is a zero-tolerance policy toward using library property for parkour. Don't worry, when this whole thing blows over, come and see me and we'll talk to Circulation and Security and figure it all out."

"Remarkable," Lovecraft cut in. "I've noticed this with young people here in Hamilton."

"What's that?" Meghan and I looked at each other.

"That group that just went by." Lovecraft spoke like a bird watcher who had just logged a particularly rare species. "The young people here – they are so racially heterogeneous. Do you know what I mean? You don't see a group that's all white youngsters, or all black, or all Oriental …"

"Actually," Meghan said, "we say *Asian.*"

"… and I wonder." Lovecraft peered at each of us intently, as if the question he was about to ask really worried him. "As these teenagers get older, isn't anyone concerned … isn't there the danger of racial … you know … *mixing?*"

Meghan and I looked at each other again. She burst into a loud guffaw.

"Mixing?" she laughed. "I love it!"

"Maybe we should go back to the table, and sit down," I said.

Meghan pointedly paid for her latte before Lovecraft could offer and we went back to the table.

I thought this might be a good time to get back on topic, to announce that as far as the Resurrection Church went, I was way ahead of these people; to tell them what had happened to Dana, and about the unusual hidden abilities and other, I-guess-you'd-call-them, features possessed by the scooter lady called the Interlocutor. But unsure of how to take charge of a conversation with two older people I barely knew, I kept my mouth shut.

Lovecraft was eating a cheese sandwich with lettuce and tomato. "I'm sure you're skeptical," he said, as mayonnaise dripped from his sandwich onto his plate, "so let me assure you that, of course, I make no claims to be the real H. P. Lovecraft – he passed away many years ago, tragically before his time – but a proxy H. P. Lovecraft. Every few years the Lovecraft Underground adjudicates a proxy Lovecraft, whose knowledge

of the Great Old Ones qualifies him to act as an investigator –
an advance scout, if you will – into the terrestrial conspiracies
of the so-called ancient gods and their agents on this planet."

"Wow," I said. "How did you get all this knowledge?"

"So you believe in all this?" asked Meghan.

"My real name," continued Lovecraft, "is Timothy Kerwin,
and believe me, I am only too eager to get back to my wife and
children in Cleveland." He finished off his sandwich, dabbed his
lips with a napkin and, I couldn't help but notice, ignored our
questions completely.

"Nate," he said, "thanks for your email. It has put the
Underground on red alert. A lot of the members, if you ask me,
have been getting complacent. Sloppy. Decided that the
Resurrection Church had given up, or even that the whole threat
is just fantasy. The Underground's membership had dropped.
The edge had gone off our vigilance. Until we got your email."

"You didn't waste any time getting here." Here it was, Sunday,
and I'd sent the email on Friday. Lovecraft had popped up in
Hamilton the very next day.

"So the Lovecraft Underground is sort of a vigilante group?"
Meghan asked.

"I prefer to think of them as researchers, separating the
phantoms and rumours of fiction from the very real evidence
that the Great Old Ones exist and are a threat."

"So, has there ever been a female Lovecraft?"

Lovecraft's eyes widened. His cup of tea stopped halfway to
his mouth.

"After all," Meghan continued, "you said every few years the
Underground chooses a proxy Lovecraft, and none of them are
going to be the real H. P. Lovecraft anyway, so why not ..."

"No," Lovecraft said. "Of course not."

"This is, after all, the twenty-first century."

"I am aware of that." There was a moment's pause. "What a
bizarre idea," Lovecraft started to say. "It seems highly unlikely
that a woman could ..."

A wave of despair swept through me, and I sank into my chair. In the past couple of days, the world around me had become a much more dangerous place. I needed help anywhere I could get it.

I sat up straight and cleared my throat. "Now just a sec, Meghan and, uh, Mr. Lovecraft. Howard. Not that gender issues aren't really important. They really are. But I need help with some things. I'd like to tell you a story, and I'd like both of you to let me know what you think about it."

"I'm here to listen," Meghan said. She looked at her watch. "But I don't have much time."

"Me too," said Lovecraft. "Ready to listen, and I have all the time in the world."

"I hope you're right," I said. "But I warn you, this is a scary story."

"Don't forget who you're talking to, young man," said Lovecraft. "Or at least, sort of talking to. If you can scare *me*, I'll buy you another muffin."

I told them about my visit to the midnight game with Dana; about the creature we'd seen, and the man it carried away; about the immense shape in the sky that had reached down from the clouds, almost close enough to touch us; about the Proprietor, the cheering and chanting crowds.

Lovecraft said, "It sounds as if the process is just starting, although I'm surprised at the appearance of that huge arthropodal creature; we call it an exanimator, although on its home planet it is known as a dritch. It seems as if Yog-Sothoth has gotten through to a few individuals, a new cult has formed and they're starting to make these tentative attempts to establish a continuum threshold between worlds – and in the process, they're enlisting new members." He harrumphed. "But that's not particularly scary. It simply illustrates one small facet of the situation we have on hand."

So I told him about coming to the library to see the *Necronomicon*, meeting Meghan and being chased by the Proprietor and his thugs ...

DAVID NEIL LEE

"Goodness," said Lovecraft. "That *is* pretty scary. Although it's nothing like what all of us would suffer if ..."

"Do you know a street person who's called the Interlocutor?" I asked Meghan.

"Sure. She asked to see the *Necronomicon* once, and I had to wrestle it off her to get it back. We all keep an eye on her when she comes into the library. The Resurrection Church types seem to all know her. Know here and hate her." She shuddered. "She gives me the creeps."

"She has tentacles."

"What's that?" asked Lovecraft.

I told them about being ambushed on the walkway by the Proprietor and his friends, and how the Interlocutor had come to my rescue.

"Are you saying she's not a human being?" Meghan asked.

"Hmm. If an Interlocutor has been assigned," said Lovecraft, "if its support group has devised a powerful enough continuum threshold to bring an Interlocutor to Earth, then things are much more advanced than I thought ..."

"Sounds gross," said Meghan.

"Aside from the tentacles," I said, "and the weird way she looks and smells ... and moves ... and talks ... she was really okay. Those people wanted to hurt me, and she stopped them. So, gross, yes, but I'm sure glad she came along."

"If you say so," Meghan said. She wrinkled her nose. "I don't think I'd want to have lunch with her."

"Her tentacles are really powerful," I said. "I wouldn't mind having a set myself."

"Be careful what you wish for," said Lovecraft. "All this really shows is that we're in a crisis that's intensifying." He offered a shaky smile. "You sound as if you're quite resourceful, but as far as a muffin goes, I'm sorry, Nathan, you just haven't earned..."

So I told them how I'd decided to crash at Dana's current crib ... how I'd scoped it out in the Prince of Wales school, condemned and abandoned ... and as I described what had happened there, I found myself getting choked up. I paused while I tried to get my voice back.

"Are you okay, Nate?" Meghan asked.

"Sure." I cleared my throat. "It's just that ... we were friends." I coughed and got some of my voice back. "Anyway, I got into the classroom, and the plywood swung shut behind me. It was pitch black, but I'd brought a flashlight. Ahead of me in the darkness I could hear ... sounds of some kind, and I smelled a stink that at first I thought was gas."

"No," I heard Lovecraft whisper.

"And there was this haze of blue smoke, and sounds coming out of the dark ... chittering sounds, like big bugs, but at the same time, it didn't sound like an animal, like something that was really *alive* ... not the way we think of what a living thing is."

I told them how it all had faded, the sounds and the smell and the smoke, and then how I'd gone through the door of the gymnasium, and found Dana bloody and headless.

I was so glad to have finished. I took a deep breath. My voice was harsh as I said, "So, if that doesn't earn me a muffin –" I tried to smile. "– I don't know what will."

Talk about mixed emotions. Lovecraft making a dare out of storytelling had cheered me up a bit. Telling this story was a challenge, and facing it made me feel better about my prospects. Meghan looked horrified, which I regretted – although at the same time I felt a faintly wicked sense of power.

Lovecraft, however, was simply staring straight ahead and not saying anything. He sat that way for about half a minute. It was starting to seem rude.

"Well, I'll just grab *myself* a muffin and another hot..." I plucked the American five off the table and looked Lovecraft in the eye to make sure he knew I was kidding around.

His face was pale as a page of the *Necronomicon*. His mouth fluttered open and he made a far-off, leaky wail, like the sound the old radiators in PoW made when the pressure changed. His hands gripped the edge of the wooden table, his knuckles white.

Meghan leaped up and started pounding him on the back.

"Breathe," she said crisply. "Howard, breathe." She looked at me. "Nate, loosen his tie."

Another thin wail came from Lovecraft's mouth. "Why is he crying?" I asked as I tugged at the knot of his blue paisley tie. Finally I was able to pull out a loop.

"He's not crying. He's trying to breathe. He's having a panic attack."

I managed to pull off his tie and loosen the collar of his buttoned shirt. Everyone was staring at us. Lovecraft gasped and started to cough. Then he took a deep rattling breath and leaned back from the table.

"Air," he said. "Some fresh air ..."

We helped him up and moved out to a table on the patio, huddling against the cold wind that came at us down King William. The grey-haired woman was gone. The man who served us from the bar came out with a glass of water, which Lovecraft took gratefully, thanking him in a thin, exhausted voice.

"Should we call 911?" the bartender said.

"Thanks," Meghan said, "but he's feeling better. He's come a long way and he's tired."

"I was worried he might have a heart problem. I'm glad the fresh air did him some good." The bartender shivered. "Today's the last day we'll have the chairs out here." He looked into the rising wind. "You can come back in if you want."

"Please, get yourself inside, it's chilly." Lovecraft handed him the empty glass. "I'm really feeling much better."

He didn't look much better. He looked haunted and aghast, and when we were alone again he said, "I had no idea that the situation in Hamilton was so far along. It might even be the case that the next of these mass rituals – the midnight games, you call them – will be the last."

"You mean they'll finally give up?"

"A few minutes ago, that's what I thought. Because most of the cults never develop the organization, the cohesion, the weight of massed intelligences that they need to make a successful continuum threshold. But if they've been able to do that here ..." He shook his head. "It's very possible that next time they'll succeed. And life on earth, as we know it, will change beyond all comprehension."

"How do you know this?" asked Meghan.

"Because from what Nate tells me, they've gained a power that is granted only to very few – only to those who have spent many years in the services of the Great Old Ones; only those who have learned much about their arcane sciences – not only to follow their blasphemous protocols, but to master their essence. Nate, to the best of your knowledge, did your friend Dana receive anything out of the ordinary in the days before his death – did he mention being given anything ..."

"Now that you mention it ..." I told them about the paper passed to Dana by the Proprietor, that translucent slip with its strange characters or symbols, and the message "allowed forty-two hours."

"Exactly," Lovecraft sighed. "My worst suspicions are confirmed. From what you have told me, Nate, they are able –" He had to catch his breath. "– they are able to summon the Hounds."

CHAPTER 15
SNATCHED

Meghan looked at her phone and said, "I don't have much time."

We all stood up, Lovecraft a bit unsteadily. I grabbed the wrapped book I'd brought in a FreshCo shopping bag and eyed him carefully, not wanting to bring on another panic attack. "So what about my muff ...?" I started to ask, but they were already out on the sidewalk. I shut up and followed them.

Meghan was the only one of us who was one hundred per cent sure where to go next. Lovecraft, still dazed, looked at his wristwatch and spoke vaguely about "making some calls." We milled about for a bit, then followed Meghan toward Jackson Square. I scanned the street, still empty on this Sunday morning. Behind us, a police car whizzed down Hughson. Up ahead, a white delivery vehicle idled at the corner of James, its hazard lights blinking.

"I've got to get back to my hotel room," Lovecraft was saying.

"What can I do?" I asked.

"Young man, you've done quite enough," he said.

"I don't think so. I think there's more." The Interlocutor had told me this, though she hadn't been specific. But she had told the creeps from the Church that I was under her protection. She had put her hand on me. I couldn't step back. Whatever happened now, I had to see it through to the end.

"We'll take over now. The Lovecraft Underground."

"LUG," Meghan said. "As in, ya big lug?"

A gust of cold wind blew into our faces.

"Can we hurry into the square, please?" She started to pull ahead of us.

As we passed the van, Clare stepped out of the entrance to the Lister Block and stood in our way. The side door of the van slid open and the Proprietor leaned out, took Meghan by the shoulders and pulled her backward. I grabbed his arm and he elbowed me in the face; it hurt so much that I let go, then suddenly someone else was shoving me into the van. Meghan drew in her breath to let out a tremendous scream, but the Proprietor punched her hard in the stomach.

"Shut up," he hissed. "You'll all get hurt and it'll be nobody's fault but your own." Lovecraft hurtled past me into the van, thrown by Jimmy with what seemed to be great relish.

Jimmy slammed the side door and got into the driver's seat. The van turned south onto James, with the three of us as stunned prisoners.

"When are you guys going to give it up?" I asked.

Meghan moaned and took a breath.

Lovecraft struggled to sit upright and look angrily at our kidnappers. "This is not what I had heard about Canadian hospitality."

"If the Underground is going to send help," I told him, "now would be a good time."

We braced ourselves as the van lurched to the left. I'd been pushed onto the engine cover behind Jimmy; where I sat I could feel the engine rev and subside, rev and subside as Jimmy negotiated the lights along Main Street. Meghan was beside me on the floor, with Clare between us, and Lovecraft was guarded, as he sat against the side door, by the Proprietor himself.

"Who the hell is this guy?" the Proprietor indicated Lovecraft. He pulled a roll of duct tape from his jacket pocket. "Let's bind 'em up." He looked at me, then at Lovecraft.

"If it's the book you want, take it," I said, reaching inside my coat and holding out the plastic shopping bag. The Proprietor grabbed it from me and pulled the book out of the bag. He scanned the name I'd written on the newsprint wrapper.

"You can't even spell. It's *NecroNOMicon!*"

"Try the other side. You can let us go now. You've got what you want."

"Perhaps," the Proprietor said. "Meanwhile, here's your bag back." He folded the brown plastic bag into a little square. "Reuse and recycle, right?" He didn't seem like a recycling type of guy to me, but without thinking I took the square of plastic from him and I put it in my pocket.

"Kid, you can go," he said, "but I think we'll hang onto your friends here."

"That's not the deal."

"I agree," said Meghan, still panting with the pain of the Proprietor's punch. "I've had enough of you people. I'm going home." She pushed herself off the floor and Clare reached for her. I grabbed at Clare to pull her away, then my head exploded and I saw stars. The Proprietor had backhanded me. I struck out at him, landing a glancing blow on the side of his chin, but he shook it off and punched me expertly in the head, and then in the stomach. I fell back onto the motor cover. Meghan had also been forced back onto the floor.

I coughed and felt tears leaking from my eyes. My head and my stomach ached.

"Lesson to you, young man," the Proprietor said. "You can struggle all you want when you reach your final destination. You don't want to spoil the fun by getting beaten to death in the van ..."

"You're disgusting," Meghan hissed.

The Proprietor ignored her. "... because we've got a new addition to the Church. A beautiful creature – it comes from deep underground. We want to keep it happy. And to stay happy, it has to feed."

"You go everywhere with your personal thugs – I'm disgusted that one of them's a woman – so you can insult and bully whoever you want whenever you want. Especially kids and women." Meghan's voice trembled and she fidgeted nervously, uncoiling her scarf from around her neck.

"Meghan ..." I blinked tears from my eyes.

"I've known losers like you all my life. The first thing you think of in the morning, and the last thing at night, is ways to hurt and degrade women."

The Proprietor sighed loudly. I was worried that if Meghan didn't shut up, she was just going to make them madder.

"Nate," Meghan said. "Howard. Why don't you grab the nearest door, and open it?"

"What?" we both said. I glanced at the door, and, as the Proprietor smirked, Meghan removed her scarf, leaned forward and hooked it over Jimmy's head. In two quick moves she knotted it once, binding Jimmy's neck back onto the headrest. The van careened to one side. Jimmy braked, but, restrained as he was, he couldn't steer properly as Meghan knotted the scarf again, before Clare and the Proprietor yanked her away. Something hammered against the side of the van. Behind us a horn honked long and loud. I heard the screeching of brakes. The Proprietor tried to put Meghan in a headlock as the van slowed, but then someone else ploughed into us, and he lost his hold. Meghan stood up and kicked Clare off of her.

Lovecraft meanwhile, rising to the occasion, had started to slide open the side door. The Proprietor swore, then we crashed into something else and he fell backward. The van stopped, and as cars and trucks around us honked, the three of us burst out onto Main Street. Lovecraft slid the door shut behind us, and we threaded our way through two lanes of fuming traffic. Running down a narrow street, where curious eyes stared at us from every other porch, we got to the next corner and stopped to catch our breath.

"Where are we?" Meghan asked. She was keying a number into her cellphone.

"Fairholt Road," I gasped. "Just east of Sherman. Are you guys okay?"

"As well as can be expected..." said Lovecraft. He shook his head. "I wonder what that was all about."

"Meghan just about got us all killed," I said. Meghan was on her phone, giving the nearest house number to a taxi service. She looked at me.

"We were in heavy traffic. We weren't going that fast. Those guys were scaring me."

"Me too," said Lovecraft. "I just wonder what in the world ..."

"They are such jerks," said Meghan. "That was my favourite scarf."

CHAPTER 16
INVASIVE SPECIES

We waited for Meghan's cab, glancing nervously back toward Main Street in case the proprietor and his creeps from the van came after us. But we only heard car horns and shouting: the chaos of the accident was no doubt sucking up every bit of their attention. After a few minutes the waiting seemed endless. Meghan suggested we walk up to the corner of Main and flag the cab when it arrived.

"No way," I said. "Go back to Main Street? I'm not getting an inch closer to that van. Let's head up to King."

"Don't worry," she said. "We thoroughly screwed them. With luck, they will all get arrested." A cab rounded the corner and came toward us.

When we got in, Meghan asked the driver to go to the library, York Boulevard entrance.

I protested. "We should go to my place!"

"I've got to go to work." She looked at her watch. "We're short-staffed on Sundays; I can't not show up."

"Can't you just phone in and tell them you've just strangled somebody with your scarf and caused a major traffic accident, so now you're on the run from a monster-worshipping religious cult?" I looked up and caught the cab driver watching us in his rear-view mirror. He looked away as soon as we made eye contact.

"I hate making excuses," Meghan said.

We negotiated that, since we were so close to my house, I would get dropped off, and she and Lovecraft would head back downtown.

"You certainly caused a mess," said Lovecraft. "We could have been hurt or killed."

"You're welcome," Meghan said. "Let's vote on what would have happened to us if we'd stayed with the Proprietor and his friends."

"Yes, you're right," sighed Lovecraft. "From Nate's description of the ceremony the other night, and from what the Proprietor said, the Church has corralled an exanimator or, to use the name from its home world, a dritch."

"Where would something like that come from?" I asked.

"It's another sign that the plans of the Resurrection Church are getting dangerously close to fruition. They've not been able to sustain a continuum threshold large enough to admit Yog-Sothoth, but their repeated efforts have enabled lesser creatures to slip through. The dritch is especially attracted to the field of a threshold, so the dritch is the most often-reported creature of any threshold-related invasive species."

"I find all of this slightly hard to believe," Meghan said.

"I don't," I replied, thinking not only of my own experiences, but of Dana's fears about the industrial north end, and what he had heard and seen from the abandoned freighter. "By any chance, are dritches amphibious?"

"Very much so," said Lovecraft. "And nocturnal, and they can burrow considerable distances underground. In favourable terrestrial environments, the dritch can achieve great size."

The cab driver muttered, "You people are crazy."

"*Dritch.* I'll believe it when I see it," Meghan said.

"When that day comes, don't get too close," Lovecraft cautioned. "We call them exanimators because they are so deadly, that on their home planet they are bred as instruments of war. They secrete a poison, which they inject to soften the flesh of their prey, the better to tear off chunks with their serrated mandibles."

Meghan said, "Maybe the Church won't be so eager to come after us now that they have the copy of the *Necronomicon.*"

"Actually, they don't," I announced. "I didn't put the *Necronomicon* inside that package I handed over. The book inside that package was perfectly suited for followers of the Great Old Ones: *Quilting for Seniors.*"

THEY DROPPED me off and headed downtown, Meghan to work and Lovecraft to his hotel. Halfway up our front steps, and there are only six of them, I stopped to rest. It had been one hell of a weekend: was it going to keep up this way, or was I going to catch a break, have a minute to think about all this and maybe get a chance to chill out?

I looked up and down the street. On the left, down the block the Rivas family clustered around their van, dressed as if they were coming back from church. A few houses to the right, Mrs. Smot was crouched in her front yard with scissors, trimming the last of her summer lawn. Nowhere could I see lurking vehicles, angry thugs or extraterrestrial supermonsters.

As I pulled out my keys a white business card fell onto the porch. I picked it up and let myself in. I carefully locked the door behind me, went into the living room and sank onto the couch.

I looked at the card.

RESURRECTION CHURCH
OF THE ANCIENT GODS
– *A CHANGE IS COMING* –
99 MARKLE AVENUE

This was the card the Proprietor had given me at the stadium. *A change is coming.* Strangely enough, it echoed what Dana had said about his nights in the abandoned freighter, hearing something brush up against the hull in the dead of night. "Something big comes out of the deep part of the lake, to tunnel under the city … something is happening … things are changing."

And those road workers I'd talked to – they seemed to think that something scary was going on under the city streets.

And that woman in the scooter, who was not really a woman or, for that matter, a creature of any recognizable gender or species. Yes, she existed; I had seen her and touched her and she had spoken to me. A change was coming, for sure.

Dana sensed it wasn't a change that meant better times. "One way or another, I'm gonna get screwed," he'd said.

I took off my jacket, went into the kitchen and looked out at the backyard. Pips the cat was nosing around the garden. There was a rustle of movement in the bamboo, another cat or a squirrel. To all appearances, front and back, life on Somerset Avenue was dead calm.

I dropped back onto the living room couch and tried to picture the city's shores. I had never been far into the industrial lands. For one thing, lots of it was fenced and barricaded: *keep out*. But why were the Great Old Ones coming back here – why Hamilton? Why the beat-up old east end? Was it all the people here who were needy and desperate, feeling ripped off by hard times? I settled into the couch and let my mind wander, scanned the city in my mind's eye. I went through our neighbourhood, expecting to soar over the industrial district and then out over the lake – over to the other side and beyond, to Toronto and then the country and then the world – but this afternoon, something was wrong. In the north end I flew out over an abyss, and suddenly my imaginary wings could find no purchase in the empty air. I was plummeting while something huge and dark curled over me like a tsunami, and I heard the words from the midnight ceremony echo in my brain – Yog-Sothoth – along with weird unpronounceable syllables, something like "fahengluey midlewuh'naf cthulhu erlieh wugah-naggled fuhtagen." I turned in my sleep, and woke up to a sound like an angry buzz that rose to a frightened screech. Groggily, I blinked and stretched. What was all that? I looked at my phone. It was mid-afternoon.

Dad would be home soon. It was up to me to start cooking. First, I'd do a few chores to wake up.

I went into the backyard and filled up the watering can. In a few weeks, it would start to get cold enough that, anticipating the first frost, we would drain the hose and shut off the faucet, but for now the water was still running.

Rocky clattered into the fence as soon as I'd come outside, so I put down the can and went to go see him. As I fed Rocky a marrow bone and scratched his head I relaxed a little bit. Out here, things were normal. I looked around for Pips, but he was gone. A rusty hoe leaned in the corner of the yard – I had been meaning to bring it in since August. A few knobbly tomatoes still bobbed in the neglected vegetable garden. Nothing here could behead anybody or, as far I knew, even wanted to; nothing here had tentacles; et cetera. Rocky was still getting fed and put out in the yard – maybe when all this stuff blew over, I would go around the corner and down Rosemont, knock on Melanie's door, apologize for the creep who'd chased me into her backyard and ask her if I could take him for a walk.

I patted Rocky one last time and went to water the overgrown bamboo stump. But it was gone.

Where Stumpy had been, there was a ragged hole in the garden, as if an abyss had opened up under Stumpy and it had simply fallen away.

I dropped to my knees and reached my arm into the hole. I felt nothing but damp, cold space: I waved my arm around and hit solid earth on every side. I pulled my arm out. This was a serious hole. Part of what the road worker implied was a wave of sinkholes in lower Hamilton. His exact words, in fact, had been, "Like there's something big down there, and it wants to come up."

I went into the kitchen and scanned the cluttered counter. I picked up an old flashlight, clicked it on and off to check that it still gave off a flickering yellow light. But what was this?

There was blood on the flashlight. It had come from me. There was dirt on my sleeves, along with the blood, from when I'd knelt on the grass and reached far into the hole, and there were more smears on my pants, along with wisps of black and white fur.

I yelped and ran upstairs to the bathroom. There was a centipede in the bathtub. I yelled in anger and stomped at it, but it dodged, skittering to one side and desperately trying to climb the tub's sheer sides. I tried to smash it with my fist but it evaded me again. I looked at the smear of cat blood my sleeve had left on the old scratched enamel. Then I took a few deep breaths, went into my bedroom, got the peanut butter jar, scooped up the wiggly bug and screwed shut the lid.

I emptied my pockets onto the floor, took off my hoodie, jumped into the bathtub and turned on the shower. The water soaked through my clothes and ran down the drain, pink and murky. I pulled the hoodie in with me, and I didn't strip off all my clothes until the water started to run clear. I scrubbed my hands until they stung. The room filled with steam. I turned off the water and squeegeed my skin with my hands, searching for the slightest leftover stain or wisp of black fur.

Wrapping myself in a towel, I took everything down to the washing machine in the basement. I dripped extra detergent on all the darker spots and put my clothes in the wash.

I shivered as I looked out at the backyard. Dammit, wasn't anything the way it seemed anymore?

I got dressed and headed back out to the garden. I spread a garbage bag in front of the hole and knelt on it. Rocky came up and pressed against the fence, eager to see what I was doing. I shone the flashlight into the hole. This time I was careful not to touch the sides.

It was deep all right, round and wide as Stumpy had been. It sloped sharply under the bamboo patch, its bottom stained with blood and tufts of Pips' fur. I tried to recreate events. A sinkhole opens up, Stumpy gets pulled underground, Pips comes over to investigate and in a few seconds he too gets sucked down into the depths. I shone the light again. That hole went seriously *down* – in fact it wasn't just a hole, it was a tunnel. How far did it go?

Watching me from the fence, Rocky whimpered with excitement. He was obviously thinking that he was in the wrong place – all the action was over in my yard.

At the farthest flicker of the flashlight, I saw movement. Something glistened across the tunnel, and then vanished to the left. So there was a cross-tunnel, and down there, something was digging. And digging and digging and digging. Digging under the streets, so that sinkholes were "popping up" everywhere. "Like there's something big down there, and it wants to come up." Digging under Ivor Wynne, and erupting out of the stadium's guts to seize that poor guy on the stretcher and drag him off to god knows where. Hiding itself in the night and the earth and the waters of Lake Ontario. Dana had prided himself on not being afraid of the dangers that lurked in the city at night, but even his voice had trembled when he described what he'd heard from his hiding place on the *Sandoval*: "Something big comes out of the deep part of the lake. To tunnel under the city."

Rocky dropped down onto all fours and started sniffing around his muddy garden. He growled.

"This is just great," I muttered out loud, leaning over the hole. "Of all the bamboo patches and backyards in all of Hamilton, Ontario, it has to come up ..."

Rocky barked twice. Something exploded out of the dirt and tackled him. He snarled, and then yelped as the thing tightened its hold and tried to pull him into the ground. I ran to the fence. Rocky was snared by green-jointed limbs that had erupted out of a hole like the one I'd just been peering into. His eyes were scared; he snarled as he sank his teeth into a green limb.

Grabbing the hoe from the corner, I jumped over the fence between our backyards, hooked it around one of the green limbs and pulled.

And got a good look at what had killed Pips and now was after Rocky. This thing hadn't sucked down the bamboo stump; it *was* the bamboo stump, or some creature that I had watered and talked to for months, treating it like a weird pet, when it was actually what Lovecraft had called a dritch. The stump was part of a long, segmented body that extended back into the ground. The branches around it, that had lengthened and thickened over the months, were legs bristly and jointed like a spider's. A row of stubs that I'd thought were about to sprout leaves were now glistening eyes, and the thing was shoving its length out of the soil to get two dripping pincers into Rocky.

Tugging with a rusty hoe on the segmented limb that trapped Rocky was doing no good. This dritch thing was strong. So I raised the hoe and smashed it in the head, denting its horny surface but not drawing any blood, or whatever flowed through its veins if it had veins. Rocky's growls had become hoarse grinding sounds as the thing's limbs crushed the life out of him. I jammed the hoe into its mandibled mouth and pushed with all my strength. The dritch didn't like that. It shuddered and out of its mouth came a sound like a busted lawn mower. HRUGAKAKKAGARRHHHH! and it pushed back.

I dug my heels into the battered grass. Turning its attention to me, its grip loosened and Rocky pulled himself away, panting and gasping. The dritch lunged at me, and I pushed back. I might as well have been trying to push away a bulldozer. It spat out the hoe and surged forward, knocking me onto my back. Its limbs closed around me. I grabbed at one but couldn't stop it from tightening. I felt the limb shudder; Rocky had bitten into its end and was tugging on it, snarling. I tried to raise my legs to kick but everything was pinned down. I could feel the cold, muddy yard under me and above me ... I looked right into Stumpy's face. Its pincers dripped greenish liquid onto my shirt. If I can just free a hand, I thought, I could punch one of its nasty cold compound eyes, punch it right off its head.

And then something made the dritch turn back toward the bamboo patch, and I was freed from its weight. With Rocky barking and growling and snapping, but keeping his distance, feinting for a quick snap then jerking away before it could grab him, the thing turned and headed back toward the fence. I pushed myself to my knees, and as the creature headed back down into its hole, I staggered after it and kicked at the cluster of limbs and feelers or antennae or whatever they were that ringed its rear end, and then it was gone. Rocky jumped up and licked me.

"Hey, Rock," I said, "we whacked its sorry ass. It won't want to deal with us again ..."

"GET THE HELL OUT OF MY YARD!"

A stout, red-faced woman in a billowy dress came out of the back door and headed toward us. Her frazzled brown hair was tied back in a ponytail and her pink, rabbit-eared slippers tick-tocked toward us over the muddy lawn. I gestured toward the hole.

"WHAT THE HELL HAVE YOU DONE TO MY YARD – LOOK AT THAT MESS – WHATCHA DONE TO MY DOG, YOU BASTARD –"

Rocky stopped jumping up on me and jumped up on Melanie, clearly (1) glad to be alive and (2) glad to see his owner and me getting on so well.

I looked at Melanie and shrugged.

"Melanie, believe it or not, it was some kinda monster, and ..." I backed up as she stomped up and shouted into my face.

"– DON'T NEED YER PERVY FRIENDS CHASIN' THROUGH MY YARD AND GETTIN' BIT. YA GO PLAY SOMEPLACE ELSE, YA LITTLE SHIT, AND STAY THE HELL OUTTA –"

I turned and, though aching in my knees and back, looked around for the hoe. It was gone.

"I SAID GET THE HELL OUTTA –"

"I can't find my hoe," I said weakly.

"DON'T CALL ME A HO, YOU SUNUVA –"

Not only had the dritch tried to eat Rocky, not only had it just about killed me, not only had it zippered back into the ground, leaving me holding the bag for the mess in Melanie's backyard, to add insult to injury it had made off with my hoe. As I jumped over the fence, leaving Melanie to fuss and fret over the pet she usually shoved out into the yard and forgot about, I said goodbye to my chances of becoming her dog-walking best buddy. I headed into the house with no illusions about whether I was beating a cowardly retreat. Oh well, I could always count on a hero's welcome from Rocky.

"– AND DONTCHA COME BACK, CALL ME A HO WILLYA, YA LITTLE PRICK. AND YOU STAY THE HELL AWAY FROM MY DOG!"

CHAPTER 17
SECRET HISTORIES

That was it for me. Life was just getting too scary. I took another shower with my clothes on. This time it hurt, because I had scrapes and bruises all over my body from my battle, if I could call it that, with the dritch. I ached all over. And I was running out of clean clothes.

Why didn't Stumpy kill me? The thing was as strong as a grizzly bear. Whacking it with the hoe hadn't made so much as a dent. If it was hungry, having eaten Pips and made a grab for Rocky, for sure it would have found me delicious. I pulled my first set of clothes back out of the dryer, the dark stains left by cat blood hardly noticeable, and threw in the outfit that had just taken a beating in Melanie's yard. Screw this. I was getting nowhere and doing nobody any good. Maybe I had just saved Rocky from getting eaten, but even if I liked Rocky and didn't want him to get eaten, that didn't mean that *I* should get eaten, did it? It was time to concentrate on stuff that would do me some good.

For that matter, since when was it up to *me* to stop the Resurrection Church of the Ancient Gods from bringing whatsisface, Yog-Sothoth, and the rest of these Great Old Ones – extraterrestrial supermonsters with names like vanity licence plates – from their world into ours? Why me?

I had a long list of priorities of my own: for example, both Dad and I need to make more money. I need to keep getting good marks, so that when I graduate in a few years, I can get scholarships and go somewhere, anywhere besides here. I need to figure out some way to ask Mehri out to a movie or something without barfing from nerves, or making her brother laugh at me, or getting in trouble with her father, who had just offered me some kind of help if I was going to have the Resurrection Church of the Ancient Gods pitted against me. "Don't ever think you're alone in this," Mr. Shirazi had said. That was a laugh – so far the only help I'd had was from my awesome running-away talents (though Meghan and her scarf had been useful). I continued my list of needs.

Getting in better shape – if I was going to keep getting assaulted by bad guys, I should learn karate or something. That brought me back to the money question.

But I made a resolution: I wasn't *going* to be attacked by bad guys anymore anyway, because I was opting out of the whole midnight games / Resurrection Church / Proprietor / Interlocutor mess. I would fill in the hole in our bamboo patch … make a little popsicle-stick cross to mark Pips' last stand. And then I would do my best to forget the whole thing. Winter was coming and when spring arrived I would break the news to Dad that we needed a new hoe.

Then I had a thought. For months I had been innocently watering Stumpy, thinking it was some kind of outsider bamboo shoot. Then one day, it had gone and eaten my favourite cat buddy. But it had given up on attacking me.

Could it be that it had *recognized* me?

WITH AN eye on the clock, I boiled some noodles and rummaged around for ingredients. "I am declaring the continuum threshold," I said to myself, "discontinuumed."

When Dad got home he cast a skeptical eye at the walnut pesto I had made, using a lot of substitute ingredients to recreate a dish I'd had at the Shirazis. He made dubious remarks about its taste, colour, nutritional value and cultural pedigree. But when he sat down to eat supper, he devoured forkfuls with enthusiasm.

"How did things go," he asked between mouthfuls, "with your meeting downtown today?"

"Very interesting."

As I tried to figure out a non-upsetting way of getting Dad up to date, the doorbell rang and I went and peeked through the curtains. The man who called himself H. P. Lovecraft was standing on our porch shifting from foot to foot and looking nervously into the distance. I sighed and held the door for him as he came in toting a backpack, a shoulder bag and a large suitcase. I helped him pile his stuff in the living room. He set it down with a sigh of relief and looked around in surprise. I was used to this reaction from visitors.

"Tapes," observed Lovecraft. "Not the discs – those are more modern, aren't they?"

Every available inch of wall space in our living room is covered with shelving holding thousands of VHS tapes, ordered alphabetically by title.

"They had to go somewhere," Dad said. "I should have sold them when I had the chance, before everyone realized that the days of VHS were gone for good. Now, they're about the only legacy I have to leave to the boy. This old house, and about a million hours of old movies."

I introduced Lovecraft. "Dad, this is Howard – he's kind of an anti–Resurrection Church guy."

I was trying to keep things simple, but I failed. Dad, at first glad to meet an anti–Resurrection Church guy – "anyone who's an enemy of those SOBs is a friend of mine" – became suspicious when Howard admitted that he was a proxy H. P. Lovecraft who had another name entirely. However, Dad offered him a chair, and Lovecraft gave us some background.

"Of course, the real Howard Phillips Lovecraft passed away decades ago: 1937 to be exact. Born in 1890, H. P. Lovecraft was long thought to be a talented fiction writer – erratic, but brilliantly imaginative, and writing in a genre that took decades to be fully appreciated. He only wrote for cheap pulp magazines – if he had lived a decade or two longer he could have seen his name on books, but he never did during his lifetime."

"Isn't that kinda sad, for a writer?"

Lovecraft shrugged. "He lived to see his name in print, time and time again, which is satisfying in itself. And he was an avid correspondent, who kept in touch with his friends, and with enthusiasts of his work, through thousands of letters. So he had a full life in many ways. Many of his correspondents went on to become well-known writers themselves, so Lovecraft's influence is undeniable. But still, he was seen as the master of a cheap and sensational genre.

"It wasn't until after World War II that people began to see more in Lovecraft's stories. In 1946, a manned rocket crashed in the Pacific Northwest – up the west coast, on your side of the border – and although there were survivors, apparently they suffered hideous fates. There were also casualties among their rescuers. It's been largely hushed up, but in documents of the crash, researchers noticed the name *Nyarlathotep*. This was evidently some form of life that they had encountered in space – a form of life that had returned with them, that had escaped when the ship crashed."

"But everybody knows the first manned space flight didn't happen until way after that ..." I interrupted.

Lovecraft sighed. "A lot goes on, that doesn't get into the official history."

I searched my memory for the facts. "Yuri Gagarin, 1961. And how could they return with a form of alien life?"

"Please, Nate, for now just trust me on this and listen."

"Where would they find alien life? *We* can't even find alien life. The Martian probes ..."

"Son," Dad interjected, "let the man talk."

I agreed to keep my mouth shut. This was exciting. Scary, but exciting.

"Over the years," Lovecraft continued, "the evidence mounted that, in fact, the world described by Lovecraft was, if not identical to our world, then more closely related than anyone had surmised. Certain facts emerged that corresponded alarmingly to what had been regarded as fiction. When the

Lovecraft Underground was formed, one of its areas of research was the correlation of events in the real world with certain events that had been presented as fiction.

"I was a fan of Lovecraft's fictional work. A huge amount of correspondence had also been published. Somehow, in the course of my reading I began to closely identify with this complex and struggling artist. It was a godsend for me to stumble upon the Underground. Every two years they elect an expert who takes on the role of Lovecraft proxy – I've just started my contract as investigator and troubleshooter – and who intercedes in situations where the Great Old Ones may be trying to break into our world. Situations such as this one."

"How are you going to stop them?" I asked.

"By gathering a vigilante force of good and like-minded people to rise up against these fanatics and disrupt the next ceremony, and if necessary the one after that, and the one after that, until they give up and this incarnation of the Church dissolves through sheer attrition."

"Just a minute here," Dad said. "You're not going to enlist my son in some kind of religious fanatic gang war."

I rolled my eyes, both at Lovecraft's mention of a vigilante force, of which I could see no evidence, and at Dad's reaction. Here he goes again, I thought. At the same time, it wouldn't pay to be too skeptical. If the bags Lovecraft had brought with him were full of high-tech extraterrestrial monster-fighting weaponry, I wanted to get my hands on some. I expected Lovecraft to say something to mollify my dad's fears, but he surprised me.

"Mr. Silva, until this morning I would have said that under no circumstances would I ask someone your son's age to join a battle this dangerous. But I'm afraid that after hearing what he has to say, I've reversed that position."

"Great." My dad's voice rose. "Who would start a war, and then put a kid like Nate on the front lines?"

Lovecraft took a deep breath. "I will do my best – I *am* doing my best – to protect your son. But I didn't put him on the front lines. He was already there, of his own volition." He turned to me. "Nate, when we were in the van today ... I'm sorry, but things moved very fast, and I'd taken a few nasty blows when they pulled us inside ... but I need to ask you ..."

"What's this about a van?" Dad asked. "You told me you went to Homegrown."

Lovecraft ignored him. "I know that you gave the Proprietor the book. But then he handed something back to you. That's what concerns me. What did he hand to you?"

"Well of course, that wasn't the real book," I said.

"What book?" Dad was getting flustered. "What proprietor? The proprietor of what?" Now Lovecraft and I were both ignoring him.

"My point is ..." Lovecraft was choosing his words carefully. "...please, Nate, just confirm with me exactly what he handed to you."

"That's simple. He gave me back the shopping bag."

"And there wasn't anything else?"

"No."

"Not a slip of paper, with strange characters on it?"

"You mean, like the one that Dana was handed after the midnight game the other night?"

He sighed. "Exactly."

"I didn't notice anything," I said, "but I'll check, if you really ..."

"Please."

My pockets were still empty from when I'd changed earlier so I headed upstairs and went through the stuff that I'd emptied out. A little pocket knife, my phone, keys, the plastic shopping bag I'd used to carry the dummy *Necronomicon* ... I grabbed the bag and took it back downstairs.

"This is all he handed me," I said. I unfolded it, and sure enough something fluttered to the floor: a slip of paper, probably a receipt from the original purchase. I pulled it out. "Look what I found."

It wasn't a receipt, it was a slip of parchment, the same as

Dana had been given the night of the games, three nights ago: it seemed about a hundred years. Now that I could get a good look at the figures on it, I could see that they were some kind of funky old symbols, or code.

And again, within their rough handwritten curves I could see angles, sharp points and holes and interstices, that shimmered like sparks in smoke, and the smoke waved and gusted into words – *In memoriam Nathan Silva allowed thirty-five hours* – and then faded away.

"What the ...?" I held the paper up to the light. The *in memoriam* message had disappeared, leaving only the strange stick-figure code.

"Isn't that the weirdest thing?" I said. "I saw my name on it, but now ..."

Lovecraft was staring at me in horror. He was getting red in the face.

"Those ... animals," he sputtered. "Worse than the monsters they serve ..."

Dad was also looking anxious. "These are, like, runic symbols, aren't they?"

"Of course they are," answered Lovecraft. "The branch of the Church that has sprung up in Hamilton is unspeakably cruel. There is no need for this savagery."

The two of them were making me nervous. I was glad when Dad changed the subject.

"So, Howard," Dad said. "Can I get you anything? Coffee, tea ..."

"Passing a parchment, and to a mere boy. Mr. Silva, I think, at this time, we should concentrate on the magnitude of this ..."

"Call me Gordon, please. Some ice cream?"

"Oh." There was a long pause. Lovecraft pursed his lips. "Well, if you insist."

"I'll get some bowls," Dad said, leaping from his chair before I could get up. Ice cream had been on sale last week and we had stocked up. Tonight, maple walnut.

"It's not the greatest ..." I said as we started.

"Oh, this is good." Indeed Lovecraft was making sincere little yummy sounds as he finished off his bowl. "This is just fine." The mood in our dining room had momentarily brightened. At the very least, we had steered Lovecraft away from another panic attack. I gestured at the parchment, which lay on the table in front of us.

"Runes are what the Vikings wrote with, right?"

Lovecraft nodded. "But many runic elements predate the Vikings. In this case, we're talking about the relationships between runes and dimensional interfaces – the infinite micro-locations where worlds may intersect, even though they enjoy their own discrete existences in different dimensions. Expert practitioners in continuum science have ways, not always predictable, of creating the conditions that enable a number of phenomena that create mini-portals, called interstices, where worlds can intersect not via three-dimensional space, but interdimensionally." He paused and looked at me. "Are you still with me?"

"Sure. Uh, whatever."

"Wait a second," Dad said. "So, this is a curse?" He waved his hand dismissively. "We're supposed to be scared?"

Lovecraft said, "Throughout the universe there are forms of life, such as life on earth, that evolved in curved space, but there are other forms of life that are very different ... that evolved in what we might think of as angled space. This form of life has evolved in a space so different from ours that their world can coexist simultaneously in time and space with ours, without either world infringing upon the other – except in rare instances where circumstances create dimensional overlaps.

"For example, when you find yourself surrounded by sharp angles – especially right angles, although what you have to watch out for are perfect right angles, which are very rare – it is not at all uncommon to feel uneasy. These are potential interstices, through which anything might slip from another dimension. Although usually different factors need to be added in order to both (a) establish a micro-threshold and (b) induce or summon any actual traveller, or entity, to cross the threshold.

"So don't wonder why, at certain places at certain times – outdoor settings with unusual congruencies of earth, wind and water; indoor settings that include a lot of right angles – you feel nervous. Such places admit conjunctions of instability – continuum breakdowns, rather than full-fledged thresholds. Especially," he sighed, "in the case of crossing runes, such as these."

"Come off of it," I said. "They're handwritten ... there's not going to be any so-called perfect right angles in them. You'd need a machine."

"I wonder if for now you could stow the theoretical stuff," Dad said, "and let me know if there's any way this might impact my son's safety, or life."

"Dad, don't worry."

"I'm afraid we have to worry," Lovecraft said. "Even a machine adjusted to the finest tolerance can't guarantee the kind of right angle, perfect to the nearest molecule, that they're looking for. However, since the earliest days of the written word, humans have known that buried within certain mingled shapes, such as runes and the most powerful of charms, are sequences of spatial relationships that can replicate the perfectly angled effect.

"Nate, according to your description, your friend Dana received a piece of paper exactly like this one on the night of the last midnight game."

"Yes, it had those same runes. Dana insisted that it had other writing on it; that at the top, it read 'In memoriam Dana Laschelles ... uh, something... forty-two hours.' But when he went to show it to me, it was gone, so I thought... Well I guess I thought he'd imagined it or made it up. Dana could be moody sometimes. But now the same thing's happened to me."

"Yes," said Lovecraft. "'Allowed forty-two hours.' And when was Dana killed?"

"Hmm ... he received that paper, or parchment, a while after midnight as we were leaving the game. And it was last night, two nights later, that I went to see him. I was hoping to crash at his squat there, just for the night. And in fact ..." I shuddered. "... I *heard* things moving in the darkness just before I found Dana. I must have got there just after..." My voice seemed to be petering out. I cleared my throat and just sat and thought.

Lovecraft nodded. "The Hounds. The Hounds of Tindalos ... well wait a second. You told me you had a copy of the book."

"I'll go get it."

"While you do that, son," Dad said. "Can I just take a look at that parchment?"

"Sure, Dad. It's right there." But my father made no move to pick it up.

"Nate, I had a heck of a shift today. I'm beat. Would you mind handing it to me?"

"Now, Gordon ..." Lovecraft began to speak, then seemed to think better of it.

I shrugged, but handed him the parchment and headed down to the basement.

I went behind the furnace, reached up to the ceiling, pried back a sheet of particleboard that covered the floor joists and pulled out the Hamilton Public Library's copy of the *Necronomicon*. I leafed through it as I came up from the basement until I found the page. "Here it is." I handed it to Lovecraft, who, at Dad's invitation, had dug our teapot out of the cupboard. While the kettle came to a boil he read it aloud:

They are thirsty for blood and humours and they are angry. The Hounds of Tindalos are aware. The winds between the stars carry to them the scent of this dimension, the world of the human, yet they cannot reach it, save if they are allowed to do so leashed by a sorcerer's corrupt physik and debased configuring. They live in a world of angles. It is only through the conjunction of perfect angles and spells they may reach us. These Hounds are driven by hate, and above all they hate, they hate those who become their masters.

"It works this way," said Lovecraft. "The cult has gathered enough energy from its followers to empower the specific runes that connect to the irradiated, toxic dimension of the Hounds of Tindalos. There is not much we understand about the Hounds except that they are perpetually angry, perpetually predatory, perpetually famished.

"Writing on parchment, skilled practitioners can configure the runes to target specific individuals. When the parchment is passed to that person, at the appointed time the Hounds will appear and – appease their hunger.

"This group must be gathering considerable power," he continued. "If its Proprietor can summon the Hounds, it's possible that his church's efforts to establish a viable continuum threshold are much farther ahead than I had assumed."

"How can I stop this?" I asked. "From what you tell me, at eleven p.m. tomorrow these things, these Hounds are going to appear, and do to me what they did to Dana."

"Son, you no longer have that problem."

"I don't get it." I looked from Dad to Lovecraft. Lovecraft explained.

"You're right, Nate, it's a genuine curse. But your father did something very brave. He asked you to pass the parchment to him, and you did. He couldn't just reach over and take it – there are protocols. That's why he insisted." He turned to Dad.

"Now, Gordon, are you prepared to hand that parchment back to your son?"

"No way."

Lovecraft sighed. "You see, Nate, he asked you for the parchment, and you gave it to him. And now the curse is transferred. At eleven p.m. tomorrow the Hounds will come not for you, but for your father."

CHAPTER 18
THE DISANGLED SANCTUARY

I shivered as I stepped out of the house. It was long after midnight, and I could feel winter creeping in through the silences of the empty street. At the end of the block a dark figure, trailing a squeaking two-wheeled shopping cart, looked back at the sound of the door opening and then vanished around the corner. I closed the front door as quietly as I could, tugging until I heard the latch click, and headed east through side streets toward the railway track.

Lovecraft, Dad and I had sat up late scheming to elude the Hounds of Tindalos. It had been done before, Lovecraft said, or there were those who said it had been done. "Or at least," he finally conceded, "there are those who say that it theoretically can be done in this way.

"The favoured method to stave off an attack by the Hounds is to line a room with putty, plaster or concrete. It has to be done carefully, rounding it off to the smallest detail to eliminate all sharp angles from the enclosing space. Without angles, the Hounds can't gain access to their victim."

"So, what do they do then?" I asked.

"Well, Nate, you would have some very angry Hounds – something I would not want to be around for. But they can do nothing but return, hissing and fuming, to the unspeakable dimension that birthed them. A dimension known only to the ancient sorcerers of R'lyhnygoth, who devised these arcane mathematics that seem, to us, to be so much like magic."

"Hey." That word had triggered a memory. "There *is* someone they call a sorcerer, who's involved with all of this somehow. The cult – outside the stadium the other night, the

Interlocutor warned that 'the sorcerer' might show up, and the Proprietor totally dissed her."

Lovecraft rolled his eyes. "I don't think we need to worry about the sorcerer. I'll explain some other time."

"But ..."

"Nate, let's focus on the business at hand, which is saving your father's life."

"If you don't mind," Dad said.

"First thing in the morning we have to go to the hardware store and purchase some kind of putty or filler that can be sculpted ... plaster of Paris, or concrete perhaps.

"Gordon, I'll need your help with this. We need to choose a room in this house that can be completed disangled – all the sharp angles must be taken out of it, to eliminate any chance of access by the Hounds of Tindalos. They can access our world only through right angles. We need to completely round off all its inside corners by filling them in with ..."

Dad thought for a moment. "Drywall compound ought to do it."

I made some tea as we sat around the dining-room table and made plans, and backup plans, to save Dad from the Hounds. The next midnight game, which might very well admit Yog-Sothoth to our world; the enlistment of thousands of hopeful, clueless people to the cause of the Resurrection Church; mass psychic takeover by an entity that wanted to remake our world into its image – all this was forgotten as we schemed to save my father from the Hounds.

Early in the conversation, Dad had offered a bed for the night: "Look, Howard, we got the room, no trouble at all," and Lovecraft had modestly declined, then accepted. Shortly afterwards he revealed that the bags he had brought were not, as I had hoped, high-tech extraterrestrial monster-fighting artillery, but simply his luggage from the hotel; which he admitted that he had checked out of, hoping that somewhere in Hamilton someone would offer him a bed.

"As luck would have it," Lovecraft sighed, "the Underground, which I'm sure you'll agree is at this moment among the world's most important organizations, is also among the least well-funded."

THIS WAS the whole idea, I thought, as the two of them sorted out where Lovecraft would sleep. The Proprietor knew that Lovecraft was in town. He had slipped me the parchment not because I was such a danger to him and his church, but because he knew that once the runes were discovered, our little cell of resistance would turn all its efforts to saving the accursed ... and away from trying to undermine his plans.

"Hamilton itself is famous for two near-misses," Lovecraft said. "In 1946 a man named John Dick almost evaded the Hounds."

"Hey," my dad said, "I know about that."

"There are those who say that in a natural setting, away from any man-made angles, the Hounds can be thwarted. Seemingly that was Dick's intention. He went out to a wild area on the outskirts of Hamilton."

"Albion Falls," Dad and I said together. He had told me the John Dick story lots of times – how as kids, his dad and some buddies were out exploring near the falls.

"There is a theory that makes more sense to me – that running water will also completely hide the victim from the Hounds," said Lovecraft. "If you immerse yourself in a current or a waterfall at the moment that the curse strikes, they will simply be unable to get at you. The shifting matrices of the moving liquid, with its dissolution of any straight lines or angles, makes access impossible. However ..."

"My dad was one of the kids who found John Dick's body." Despite the danger he was in, Dad sounded excited. This was family legend.

"It was Evelyn Dick, who did it," I said. "His wife. It was her claim to fame. She shot her husband and cut him up into bits, and she buried her baby in concrete."

Lovecraft blinked and thought hard. "People really think that? No one realizes she was trying to save …" He shook his head. "Oh well, another time." He shook his head again. "Gordon, I have no faith in the running water solution. If you wait until the Hounds appear, you won't have time to immerse yourself, and if you immerse yourself beforehand, you could drown."

"The falls are really shallow," I pointed out, "but I have another idea."

In the basement, I reminded Dad, we had an old storage drum made of stout cardboard with metal rims. It was easily big enough for a man to huddle inside. At the moment, it was full of old pillows and bedspreads, but we could empty it out in a second.

"Why don't you just plaster that," I said. "Round off all the angles inside it. It's small, so it won't take much compound – and it's a cylinder anyway. You'll just have to fill in the top and bottom."

We went downstairs to look at the drum. "A very sound idea," said Lovecraft. He peered inside the cardboard drum. "There won't be a point or a straight line anywhere. It won't take more than an hour or so to completely disangle this enclosure!"

"I just hope it'll work," Dad said.

AS THEY talked and talked, I formulated a plan of my own. I bowed out of the conversation and went to bed, falling onto my pillow and lying there like a rock for several hours. Then, as the house fell silent, I awoke anxious and full of nightmares, wondering if I would ever again sleep the whole night through.

The first part of my task was easy. Dad slept with his bedroom door open, his clothes draped over a chair at the foot of his bed. I tiptoed in and, without even needing the flashlight I'd brought, found his shirt pocket and removed the parchment I'd seen him put there.

Back in my room, it didn't take long to copy the runes with a felt pen onto a blank sheet of paper, then crop it with an exacto knife so that in a few minutes I had what I thought was a fairly decent copy of the parchment. I put the copy and the original side by side and gave myself credit: granted my lack of arcane knowledge, I was pretty sure my replica didn't have the weight of trans-continuum whatchamacallit or Hound-summoning angles, but it looked pretty darn close to the original. I crinkled the copy a bit to make it look well-travelled and then, congratulating myself that luck was on my side, I tiptoed into Dad's room and put the copy in his pocket.

I had reclaimed the parchment, and hopefully the curse that went with it, because in the next – I glanced at my phone – twenty-one hours, without Dad or Lovecraft suspecting a thing, I planned to pass that parchment back to the person who had given it to me, back to the Proprietor himself.

MY MIND made up, I headed through the night streets with only the vaguest plan of how I was going to do this. The absolutely vaguest plan. In fact to be honest, I had no plan. I was heading to the Church's headquarters out at the end of Markle Avenue. I was hoping that, with another ceremony in the offing, the place would be full of people and I could slip in and – now this would be tricky – get close to the Proprietor without him noticing me and also – this would be *really* tricky – hand him the parchment without being stopped by Clare or Jimmy or some other minion or bodyguard, and have him accept it, to willingly take it from me.

This last, in particular, was clearly impossible and I was not sure why I was even trying to do it. Mere hours ago I decided to simply ignore the Church and let the apocalypse come, or not come, without me. But now they had set the Hounds of Tindalos after me, hoping that in twenty-one hours the same thing that befell Dana would befall me. I couldn't choose to remain a bystander; like it or not, I was in this up to my neck. I looked down at my body and my clothes and my legs and my feet, taking me closer and closer to the Church. Clearly impossible ... stupid and dangerous ... no proof it would work, et cetera ... but somehow I kept walking.

I thought of Lovecraft or whatever his name was, the Underground's proxy Lovecraft. Some troubleshooter! Just when the situation called for a steely-eyed mercenary impervious to pain, preferably with a bionic arm, someone who would kick some serious butt, the Underground had sent us a nervous, gentle eccentric. A harmless goof with a weakness for ice cream. I would let him and Dad fuss over that barrel, and Lovecraft could message the Underground, which was clearly, as Meghan had thought, a geekfest, while I went out and actually did something.

CHAPTER 19
EVIE

I headed down Primrose toward the railroad tracks. I wondered if I should even be taking this route, which went right past the Shirazis' house. What if someone was up late, looked out the window, saw me and called out? Where would I tell them I was going, what I was doing?

As it happened, I could see that all the lights in the house were on as I approached.

I stopped and looked across the street. From where I stood, looking through the window of the front door, I glimpsed Sam's sister Hamideh. Well, they are a family and they have their own problems, I thought. This is not a night to drag them into mine.

As I was about to turn away, I saw another figure through the front door: a tall blonde woman, who entered the frame of the window as she stooped to hear something Hamideh was saying. She looked familiar to me.

In fact, the woman looked a lot like Meghan.

I looked both ways. The street was silent, and everyone in the Shirazis' house looked intent on their own affairs. I crossed the street to get a closer look. Hamideh left to go into the dining room, and I got a better look at the blonde woman as she followed her. It *was* Meghan.

What the hell was going on here? I turned and stomped off toward the tracks. Why did all these people seem to know each other, and yet never manage to tell me? Was I not asking the right questions? Is this what my whole life was going to be like? Standing outside, looking in at the people who were actually doing the important stuff? Was I fated to be some kind of perpetual outsider?

"Dammit," I muttered. "Here we are, Dad and I, putting our lives on the line, and nobody tells me anything ..."

I had a thought. Last night – actually in the wee hours of the morning – Mr. Shirazi had given me a card. I had never looked at the card. Now, I found it in my wallet and pulled it out, peering at it in the glow of the nearest street light.

THE LOVECRAFT UNDERGROUND
Since 1974
Defending Humankind
From the Outer Dark

There was a web address, and the familiar phone number in Mr. Shirazi's handwriting.

Hmm, maybe I had been too quick to dismiss LUG.

Still, I had important stuff to do at the Church. I turned to continue on my way. Then, from inside the Shirazis' house, I heard a woman scream.

My first impulse was to run away from the house, to continue on my own quest to save my father and disable the Resurrection Church. But I did the opposite – I ran toward the house. I was almost at the front steps when I saw movement in the kitchen, the front door flew open and a running figure threw itself down the front steps. Before I could step aside we collided and, although I pulled away, the person clung to me desperately and cried out in a high, thin voice like a seabird.

"Help me." It was a woman. She looked into my eyes.

"Nate?" Sam called from the porch. "What are you doing here?" In a moment we were surrounded, and the woman pulled back from me, darting her head around and looking more birdlike than ever. Then she looked into my eyes again, this time recoiling in horror.

"My vision," she cried. "It's come to pass."

"Evie, you'll wake up the whole neighbourhood," Sam said. "Nate, what are you doing here?"

I began to tell him, but his sister Hamideh shushed me and hustled us all into the house. There was much fussing over the woman named Evie. She sat at the table trembling, and refused repeated offers of tea.

Meghan spoke up. "I didn't know you knew the Shirazis."

"I didn't know *you* did."

"Of course I do," Meghan answered. "Mehri's been part of my English for New Canadians class since she was like, twelve. I practically couldn't run it without her.

"But I just thought of something," she continued. "This man you said you saw killed: what did he look like?" From a file folder she pulled out a photocopied poster, with a picture of a round-faced, dark-haired man grinning nervously at the camera.

Have you seen this man? Dusko Bibanovic. Age 43.

I shrugged. "That could be him. Or not. When I saw him, he was a long way off. And he was definitely not smiling."

"Dusko came to our ESL classes. He was a sweet guy with a sad story. A carpenter, brought here from Serbia by a gang claiming to be legitimate contractors. But for more than a year they kept him locked in a basement, only let out to work building condos, every day for no money. He spoke hardly any English, and they told him that if he escaped, either the cops would throw him in prison, or the gang would catch up with him, which would be worse. Finally the gang was busted, and Dusko was set free, but he had no job, was fighting deportation, trying to learn English. Then, two weeks ago, he stopped showing up for English class. No one's seen him since." Meghan started pacing the room.

"Like I said, it might be him."

"Someone else who was there, was certain it was him," Mehri said. "They told my father, and I told Meghan."

Meghan's voice came from behind me. "Nate, you're not the only one who's snuck into one of the midnight games, without being a member of the Church."

I turned to face Meghan, leaned closer to her and whispered, "So who is this lady, Evie?"

"She came to the library this afternoon, claiming she would do anything to disrupt the midnight games and looking for the *Necronomicon*. I told her she was too late, then I invited her here tonight. I'm not sure it was such a good idea."

"When my parents went out," Mehri added, "Evie suggested a seance."

"A seance?" I was dumbfounded.

"We joined hands around the table," Meghan said, "and Evie said she was feeling contact; that a message was coming to her from the dead. And then she screamed, and ran out."

"I'm so glad you were there to catch her," Mehri said.

A car pulled up outside, and Mr. and Mrs. Shirazi came in the front door. Unlike the others, they didn't look remotely surprised to see me. Mrs. Shirazi was carrying a long, wooden shovel handle, and her husband had some kind of apparatus that he laid out on the kitchen table across from where Evie sat looking at it, and him, and us, with a skeptical eye.

"Nate, just in case Howard's scheme doesn't work, this could be the way we save your father."

"Mr. Shirazi, I just looked at your card. So, you're part of the Underground?"

"Howard has been keeping me up to date." He gestured at the device on the table. "With this, we will send the Hounds of Tindalos running and whimpering like frightened jackals, their tails between their legs."

It was unlike anything I'd ever seen, its dull metal housing blinking with LED operating lights and its long point curving into a hook. "A Delphic scythe," said Mr. Shirazi. "Iron alloyed with a nickel atom fused at trapezohedric bonding angles that disrupt Tindalosian body chemistry."

I was not inclined to ask for more details. "What's it do?"

He and Mrs. Shirazi were busy fitting the scythe onto the end of the shovel handle. With a few boosts from an electric drill, Mr. Shirazi fastened it firmly in place.

"It's a weapon effective not only against the Hounds of Tindalos, but against the dritch." He smiled when I looked surprised. "Nate, I've already told you how much I despise the old H. P. Lovecraft, the author of all those stories. But this new, proxy Lovecraft – this guy really kicks ass!

"Respect your father," he snarled when his son and daughters laughed at his turn of phrase, but they only laughed again. He ignored them. "This proxy Lovecraft – Howard – has told us that you have been passed the runes, and that your father persuaded you to pass them on to him."

"Tricked me, actually."

"He did what any father would do. But there is a chance we can save him." He hefted the scythe in the air. "Stand back, everyone." He pressed a trigger wired to the end of the handle.

Looking like the beak of some huge robot bird, the Delphic scythe hummed and the air around it shimmered, like a mirage on a hot day.

"Although from here, we feel no heat," Mr. Shirazi explained, "the scythe can deliver a serious burn to normal flesh, such as ours, or the flesh of the dritch. But when it contacts a creature such as one of the Hounds of Tindalos, it completely disrupts its links to our dimension. Its molecules drop out of our space, and return to its own. The Hound will literally disintegrate on contact." He switched it off.

"Frankly, Mr. Shirazi, you know a lot more than I thought you did about the Church and the games at the stadium."

"Someday, I'll tell you why. But, Nate, look at the time. We have a long day ahead, and then a great battle."

"I guess so," I said. "I'll see you there."

"It is not for boys. Go home, Nate. Help your father and Howard prepare."

"Yes, go home." Evie spoke up from her place at the table. Suddenly I realized I had seen her before. When I had met Meghan and Lovecraft at the Homegrown, Evie was the skinny, grey-haired lady sitting outside, nursing a coffee. But when we came out, she had gone.

"I'm sorry I upset everyone," she said. "But that's me. I've always upset everyone – just by doing what I do and by being who I am." She turned her gaze on me. "You look like a nice enough kid – I don't know why you're smack in the middle of this, but you are. I saw it. If Yog-Sothoth gets through to this world tonight, if he makes it, you will be smack in the middle. His mind-control stuff doesn't work on you, does it? Me neither." She shrugged. "I'm an independent thinker, always have been. And look where it's got me." She chuckled.

"But you, son, if that monster gets through, he and his followers will do whatever they can to wipe you off the face of the earth. You, and anyone else who doesn't get on the bus."

"So, if you've seen the future," I asked, "do you know how it will turn out tomorrow?"

Evie shook her head. "Yeah, it would be so easy if I could. Sonny boy, powers like mine are just a mess. 'Cause I saw you, I really did, I saw you there, in the middle of the holocaust that will happen if the Great Old Ones are let through. But I also saw what will happen if they don't get through."

"That's great." The thought cheered me up. "Peace, love," I snuck a glance at Mehri, "and prosperity?"

Evie snorted. "What a nice, naive, optimistic young man you are. No, they might not get through, but if they don't, they won't stop trying. And you might get so tired and scared you'll want to turn your back on it, but you won't. It will just keep getting harder. And mostly you'll feel like you're all alone. But you won't be."

I looked at the clock on the kitchen stove.

"Look, I've got to go," I said. "But there's a question maybe you can answer. Every now and then someone mentions this other person: the sorcerer. Is this somebody you know about? Is he or she any use? I mean, is this 'sorcerer' someone who has any actual power? Or is the sorcerer just somebody who does magic tricks?"

"No way." Before she fell silent, retreating into her own thoughts and memories, Evie drew her feet up onto the chair, and buried her face in her knees. "The magician does tricks, the witch and the wizard bend science to gain power, for good or for evil," she said. "A sorcerer is something quite different. A sorcerer moves between worlds."

CHAPTER 20
THOSE WHO WOULD DESTROY US

I left the street lights and headed down the railroad tracks through the darkness. The railroad tracks were built along with Hamilton, for the steel industry, and a century and a half later here they were, anachronisms in more ways than one. As the industry faded and the highways got clogged with big trucks, there were fewer and fewer trains. But in another way, the tracks were like wounds carved into the body of the earth that the city was built on. Wounds that had never healed because, even when everything around them was paved, the tracks remained, unhealed and oozing untended weeds that grew into trees and bushes, hiding places for wild creatures that eked out an existence in the silences between trains: creatures that rejoiced and thrived as the trains became fewer and those silences got longer and longer. But the tracks had a lot of history, and back at PoW some kids even claimed to have seen ghost trains: black freights, unscheduled and unbranded, that came and went in the dead of night, rumbling past the houses of unhappy sleepers as they passed, forcing late-night drivers to screech to a halt as, without warnings or signals, the black freights crossed little-used intersections at reckless speeds.

Where the tracks crossed Barton I looked both ways, but traffic was light. I crossed the road like a creature of the night, unseen by the thousands of people sleeping or driving or drinking the night away in every direction. I briefly bobbed into the lights of Barton and then sank back into darkness again, following the railway cut toward Markle Avenue.

Maybe I had miscalculated, I thought, and the Church too would be silent. Even the brain-dead slaves of alien gods have to sleep sometime. But as I approached Markle, headlights crossed the tracks. I dodged their beams and crept through the bush to see what was going on at the old chain factory.

Sure enough, the place was surrounded by a shiny new chain-link fence, with a guard at the gate to check incoming cars. I frowned when I saw that instead of fencing over the railway tracks, there was another gate installed there, padlocked but just as shiny and new: why would there be a gate? Why would the Church still have freight cars rumbling into its beat-up old loading dock?

These questions didn't concern me as much as the question of getting inside and finding the Proprietor. I started to circle around the Church, picking my way carefully through the undergrowth outside the fence. I was poked by branches, and thorns tore at my clothes. When I saw a clearing open up ahead of me, I gratefully lurched toward it, only to have my right leg sink into the ground up to the knee.

Quicksand was my first thought, thinking of all those old Tarzan movies I'd seen, but all I'd stepped into was loose dirt. Someone had been digging there. Or … I thought of my run-in with Stumpy. Even if the midnight games failed, even if we managed to outmanoeuvre the Hounds, the city of Hamilton was riddled with tunnelling dritches of different sizes and dispositions. Who was going to deal with them?

I stepped back from the hole and once again pushed into the bush, trying not to make too much noise.

Behind the Church, it was dark and deserted. I couldn't see a security camera anywhere; it looked as if the only surveillance was from the guard at the front gate.

I pulled out a pair of soft leather gloves. This was a technique Dana had told me about. "If you look hard, you can find a pair of cheap ones in any Goodwill," he said, "and here's what you do …"

Basically, the gloves are for protecting your hands when you climb chain-link fences. This had been one of Dana's significant survival skills. He had also walked around town with a pair of cowboy boots tied to his backpack: he only put them on when he needed to fit their narrow toes into the diamond openings of the fence wire.

I didn't need to worry about that. Until at least my next growth spurt, which, I was sure, would begin any day now, I could get an efficient purchase just with the toes of my running shoes. All the same, using the gloves, I did my best to pull my weight with my hands and arms, taking deep breaths and moving slowly and deliberately so that I made it up the fence with a minimum of clatter. Fortunately the Church hadn't topped the fence with barbed wire or razor coil. Getting over the top was tricky but I figured it out and dropped to the ground. I could get good at this. I ran toward the Church to hide myself in its shadow.

A minivan came through the front gate and pulled into the corner of the yard, which was already filled with cars. I crouched in the darkness and watched. These people looked like normal working-class families with mums in ponytails, dads in Ticats jackets, kids in hoodies. I slipped around the corner and joined the crowd as the door opened, and in a moment I was inside.

Even at this time of night, the Church had a full house. At one side of the room there were snacks and coffee urns. At the other side, a stage draped with the church's name, that familiar logo and the lines from a poem:

And was Jerusalem builded here,
Among these bright and shining mills.

The crowd was excited and rackety. At the other end of the room, someone would occasionally bang a hammer or run an electric drill. Several Church members were putting the finishing touches on an enormous metal door that, from the raw timbers around it, had just been installed. They worked in a pool of sawdust where something dark had spilled, something that also stained the door. To the side, there was a pile of junk metal and plastic that seemed to be attracting vandals like flies: every few seconds someone would kick it or rip a piece off it.

I didn't know what I was doing, and I had the feeling that I *looked like* I didn't know what I was doing. I kept moving through the crowd, trying to get my bearings. A tall guy with a crewcut and a white jacket, embellished with the Church logo, was leaning against a wall. I caught his eye just for a second, but he started weaving through the crowd toward me.

There was a familiar figure in front of the stage: Kara. That girl just kept turning up. She seemed to be with the Church every step of the way, but right now, as White Jacket got closer, she was all I had. I made my way to the stage and greeted her.

"Nate – I'm surprised to see you here!"

"Heck, I can't really miss this." I grinned like an idiot. "Tonight's the big night."

"How's things up the Mountain?"

"You know, same old same old. Fell asleep the other day and had a dream about Yog-Sothoth."

Kara leaned forward and whispered. "They said you were on the other side."

I looked around. Seeing the two of us chatting like old buds, the guy in the white jacket was moving away. "I came around," I said to Kara. "You'd have to be nuts not to want what the Great Old Ones are offering. More jobs, better government … thank goodness for the Resurrection Church."

She frowned. "That's funny, because, watching how these people work … I've been starting to have a few doubts."

"No way," I said. I was getting into this. "I think the Proprietor's the greatest. Is he here tonight?"

She looked around. "You mean Raphe? Oh sure, he's somewhere."

"Right – Raphe." I dipped my head in an awkward gesture to signify embarrassment – and also to keep Kara's face between Clare and me as she slipped past us through the crowd. Just as she glanced my way, the lights went down and loud music started up as a spotlight was turned on the stage.

THE FIRST person to step into that circle of light was, to my surprise, the Proprietor's henchman Jimmy. He stepped up to the microphone and adjusted it.

"And now ..." he started, but the music – some kind of hurray-for-us, Star Wars–type orchestral music over an electro beat, with a chorus of girls' voices – was too loud. Jimmy gestured toward the sidelines and the volume went down.

"And now," he began again, "I know we've all worked hard for this day. And this day hasn't really started yet. We thank you all who came to help with this crisis ... or really it's just a glitch ... or a dritch ...!" Jimmy flashed a desperate-looking smile when he made this last remark. No one else seemed to get the joke; I sure didn't.

"Of course," he continued, "that dritch *was* a glitch. It's really nothing to worry about. Nothing can stop us now!" This time, he got a few whoops from the crowd, and scattered applause.

"I remember that first time I came to this church. I was looking for hope. And I found out about the ceremony – the midnight ceremony that the Church has been repeating since the summer, each time building its strength, building its heart, building its goals ..."

"The heart of the Hammer!" somebody yelled, and there were cheers.

"When I went to my first ritual I thought, what the hell is going on? I know a lot of you felt the same – we'd been told something big was coming, but where was it? But that night I came – it was only in July – that was the first night we approached success, the first night our combined energies actually summoned the great Yog-Sothoth, the first night that many of us got his awe-inspiring message. The first night we got a hint of the glorious rapture that will be life on earth, once the Great Old

Ones are returned to power!"

This time he got a big cheer. Even Kara, who had just revealed to me that she had doubts about the Church, was clapping and smiling with evident sincerity, and I could see that Jimmy himself was getting into it. I admired the graceful way he pronounced *Yog-Sothoth*. That name was a real mouthful.

"Also on that big night – a night that changed my life – I met the man who is responsible for all of us being here tonight. A man who wouldn't stop searching and questing. The man who has been anointed as the Proprietor by the Great Old Ones themselves, by Yog-Sothoth and the giant sleeping god Cthulhu, and by the dreaming of the vanished Nyarlathotep, our saviour from the stars; anointed by them to care for their kingdom on earth, as the Proprietor. I'm literally thrilled to pieces to have the honour to introduce him. Please welcome our beloved leader, the man we know as the Proprietor – *Raphe Therpens!*"

Conscious of the paper in my pocket, I joined the crowd in a tremendous ovation as the Proprietor strode to the stage, shaking hands and stopping to talk with a group here, and a group there, and slap the shoulders of the workmen. He waited a second for Jimmy to finish adjusting the microphone, then they embraced each other in a fat showbiz bro-hug and the Proprietor turned to face the crowd.

"Thank you, my friends – more than friends, my family," he said as the applause died down, and then he paused. There was a flower display next to Kara, so I buried my nose in a flower as the Proprietor surveyed the room.

"We are near the end of a long road. The road began for me one night, years ago and many miles from here. I was home after a long day, a long day in the law profession, a profession where I fought every day for the freedom to give our citizens access to our country's great resources, to protect the jobs of working people such as yourselves. I was dedicated to my profession, but until that night I had no idea that dedicated as I was, that profession was not my true calling.

"I remember I stayed up late that night, because when I looked up, the night sky was full of falling stars. Meteors – the heavens reaching out to us. Somehow, that was a special night. Somehow, without a continuum threshold or a church or a following to guide me, another world came very close to me, reached out. That night as I slept, I was visited by the Great Old Ones themselves. I heard their message. Those of you who have been to our ceremonies – especially the last one, that was a doozy, wasn't it? –" the crowd laughed "– you know what it's like when you hear that voice. It's warm and comforting. It's not a god you read about in some book; it's a very real god, a god who truly loves you. It's a voice like you've never heard, it's *the* voice. The voice you've been waiting to hear all your life. It's the voice of … the Great Old Ones."

A stout middle-aged woman was threading through the crowd. I was afraid she was looking for me, but then her eyes lit on Kara, who was right in front of me, and she bustled toward us. As the Proprietor continued to speak she caught Kara's attention, speaking in a loud whisper.

"I been looking for you everywhere! Kara, you're flower girl tonight. Take these."

They put their heads together and began picking a bouquet out of the assortment on the stand. I had an idea and thought I should stick close by.

"It's been a long night," the Proprietor was saying, "we've averted what could have been a major problem. In fact, we've killed two birds with one stone, since that horrible creature, that big shellfish-thing on the scooter, should keep the dritch from getting too hungry before tonight's ceremony. We've eliminated a major opponent – someone from the world of the Great Old Ones who thought she was being left out, who would stop at nothing to hurt us – even to strike at Yog-Sothoth himself –" the crowd hissed its disapproval "– and keep us from the glorious rapture that's knocking at the gates of heaven itself to land at our very door." While Kara and the flower woman turned away,

I plucked a single red rose from the remaining flowers and wrapped the slip of paper around its thorny stem.

"But now ... I want you all to be ready for the biggest night of your life. Go home, congratulate yourself on a job well done, get some sleep ... and get ready for a new life that starts tonight!" The Proprietor raised his hands and the crowd erupted in more cheers. He moved away from the microphone and to catch him before he left the stage, the flower woman ushered Kara to the front of the room, brandishing before her a large bouquet of multicoloured blooms. I stayed close to Kara and kept my head down.

Up on stage, the Proprietor and Jimmy shook hands and embraced. The Proprietor reached the steps just as Kara got to the bottom. Seeing the approaching tribute the Proprietor bowed, faced the crowd and reached down. Kara skipped up to the top step and extended the bouquet.

I came in close, shadowing Kara among the crowd. The bouquet was between the Proprietor and me. His hands came closer and I jumped up and pushed the rose toward his fingers. Thinking it was a straggler, he gingerly picked it up, careful of the thorns, as he took the bouquet and beamed at Kara. He gestured her up on stage. Then his eyes met mine and his face clouded over.

He pushed Kara to one side and dropped the bouquet. Remaining in his hand was the one red rose, the parchment slowly unwrapping and flapping in his hand. I waved bye-bye and started for the door.

"Why you little ... *stop him!*" The tremble of horror in his voice was satisfying to hear, but I didn't stop to enjoy it, threading my way through the crowd as fast as I could. I had passed him the runes just as everyone was ready to relax and go home and they paused when they heard the Proprietor's voice. I burst from the crowd into the open space near the front door, when suddenly someone caught my arm. I pulled and heard the fabric of my hoodie rip, then I was free. I lunged toward the door –

– and at least two people tackled me and we piled onto the hard concrete floor. I had the wind knocked out of me and tried to struggle to my feet. But there was a big guy on either side of me, and neither of them were letting go. When I tried to scramble away they just lifted me off my feet as they towed me back to the stage where the Proprietor, now laughing and smiling, gestured them to bring me up next to him.

"You think you're so funny!" he had the microphone in his hand and gave me a noogie with the other, hard. It hurt, especially because he still had the rose in that hand. He dropped it on the stage and held up the parchment.

"Let go of me," I said. The guys were squeezing hard onto my arms. In the crowd I saw laughing faces, Kara looking horrified, then more laughing faces.

"Here's the perfect end to a perfect evening," the Proprietor announced. "This little bugger has been a thorn in our side since the last ceremony. When we warned him off, he ignored us – and a friend of his died, died horribly. When we tried to claim a book that was rightfully ours – the blessed *Necronomicon*, my friends – he stole it. He plucked it from our trusting hands and kept it for himself. When we confronted him, he called for help from those who would destroy us. He called upon the monster who calls itself the Interlocutor – he'll see how we got together and squashed that bug. He called upon the fiends who he thinks are his friends. And you know what? I think friends should be together." He turned to the men holding me.

"Throw him in the vault."

As they dragged me to the back of the room, the Proprietor shouted, "Empty his pockets. No weapons. No phone." I tried to turn around to look at him, and saw that the pile of garbage I'd noticed before was an electric scooter, a lot like the Interlocutor's. "And now, just as we enter our finest hour, this white trash tries to put a curse on me. *A curse.*" Then I saw the tubes and bags, the splash of black blood. It *was* the Interlocutor's chair.

I craned my head back as much as I could. The Proprietor was holding the parchment over his head. Then I was thrown

onto the floor and kicked. Hands went through my pockets. I
heard my phone go skittering across the floor and crack against
the wall. A pen, a pocket knife, my wallet ... when they had pretty
much gone through my pockets like rats through a pizza box,
they hauled me up and dragged me toward the steel door.

"These are mystical symbols ... mathematical codes ... that
only the most esoteric, the initiated, know about. For a second I
thought the little bastard had me." The Proprietor's eyes locked
onto mine, and he raised his voice. I heard the steel door open.
I was about to find out whatever they kept in the vault. "But it's
a fake. Some phony has done this up with a ballpoint, on dollar-
store bond. The parchment is a fake."

"No, it's not," I said weakly.

"He thinks he can trick me. Well we've got a dritch we've
gotta keep happy, so let's see him trick a dritch!" The crowd
roared its approval. The side of my head bashed against the door
as it was swung open. I tumbled down wide wooden stairs,
landing on a dirt floor, and the door slammed shut behind me,
plunging me into darkness, along with whatever was down there
with me.

CHAPTER 21
TRICKADRITCH

Black as it was, I saw bright spots in front of my eyes, and when I tried to stand, the spots and the whole dark universe behind them whirled and spun. I fell to my knees and vomited onto the dirt floor. They've given me some kind of disease, I thought. Then I crawled a few feet into the darkness and collapsed.

When I opened my eyes next, they were starting to get used to the dark. I raised my head and, although it ached, I wasn't so dizzy. I groped around and my hand found a step. It rattled when I leaned on it. From up where I thought the door should be, I could hear nothing; not a voice or a creaking floorboard. Either everyone had left awfully fast, or I had been on the floor longer than I thought. I was sure cold. I tried to pull myself up off the floor. It wasn't easy; I hurt all over where I'd been punched and kicked as part of my welcome to the Resurrection Church.

I looked up at the door. Now I could see a razor-thin line of light around the frame. It seemed an awfully long way away. There was no other light in the basement except a dim patch of bluish luminescence against one wall, like a pile of dirt full of glowing worms. The stairs felt broad and dusty, made of the big thick timbers they used back in the old days. But it was cold down in this basement and I hugged myself and tried to get warmer. I could use some resurrecting myself, I thought. In a minute I would try to stand up.

I reviewed my options. I had no idea how long I'd been lying there. Upstairs, for all I knew, everyone was gone.

"Trick a dritch," the Proprietor had said. I had learned a lot in a short time. *Great serpent* – why did that phrase stick in my head? Because it sounded like Raphe Therpens, which it turns out, was the Proprietor's actual name. I had learned they had done something bad to the Interlocutor, beat her up or killed her maybe. And there was a dritch involved.

But the basement was still and silent. Nothing came bounding, drooling and snarling out of the darkness. More lies and fantasies from the Church. I closed my eyes. Then out of the dark I heard something: a wet flopping sound like a beached whale struggling to get back to the water. I opened my eyes and, accustomed to the darkness, the blue luminescence looked brighter. As I watched it moved, and from it came a dripping, shuddering sound like a lung collapsing. But it was a sound that made sense to me: "Nate ... Silva ..."

Feeling sore all over, I got to my feet, groping ahead for hidden obstacles. But the basement had an empty sound. Its ceiling seemed pretty high, and there was not so much as a cobweb. Occasionally my shoes brushed against rocks or chunks of earth.

The Interlocutor leaned back against the wall. Much of the clothing that swaddled her had been torn away, leaving expanses of pale, pebbled skin. Below her short, humanoid arms, I saw her lumpy body was framed by four enormous tentacles that lay draped around her, like the necks of a defeated hydra. In the twilight glow of the creature's luminescence, a gout of blood oozed from a wound in her upper left tentacle, near the shoulder.

"What have they done to you?"

"They have entered that country where *negotiation* means to betray and to kill. I came here alone. I hoped we could speak, before it was too late ... but there were so many of them. That human whose knife I took ... he is so angry ..."

While she spoke I took off my hoodie and the shirt I was wearing under it, shivering as I stripped. "This is all I got," I apologized. I folded the shirt and, leaning over the Interlocutor, tied it around her tentacle – which was so thick, there was barely enough shirt left for me to make a knot – in an attempt to bind the wound and stop that awful-looking gore from seeping out of it.

When I was done I was shivering, and got my shirt and hoodie back on as fast as I could. The Interlocutor saw me shiver.

"You lay still so long, I feared your death," she said. "Lean against me."

Even half a metre away, I could feel the heat that radiated from her along with that sickly blue glow.

"We've got to get out of here and get you help," I said. "Look, it probably means you'll get exposed to the public. People will have to find out. But you're cut and beaten. There must be something that a doctor can do, a human doctor."

"I cannot be looked at ... no exposure!" She shook her head. "There are made ... provisions. If we can reach my chair."

"I saw your chair. It's wrecked."

"Something hides there." She told me where to find it on the chair. "Help is waiting for me to summon. They were so excited, the people here. They moved fast, with anger. There is an alarm for help, but they were on me so fast."

"Like, a panic button?"

"If pressed, help will come quickly. There is people, mostly people, they are a squad to help me, a team. But ... the violence came so fast. They wanted my blood. But then the dritch emerged, it surprised them."

"Where'd the dritch go?"

"Its burrow is there." She gestured weakly. She gasped and fought to take her next breath. In the dim light, even in her weakened condition, her tentacles would not stop moving: they squirmed to keep her balanced, they made gross, boggy intestinal noises, they throbbed and squelched.

"I don't understand anything," I said. "What are you anyway? Why did you come here?"

The Interlocutor leaned forward and sniffed the air between us. "For a young one, you have been very close to death. Do you think that you have any hope if it has gone this far – if they can summon the Hounds? Do you think their victory can be avoided?" She sucked in air slowly and painfully, as if the body I saw before me was a poorly made machine.

"What are you?" I repeated.

"I am a border creature."

"What do you need from me?"

"There is another of us here. Soon, the dritch will return."

"Don't worry," I said. "I will kick its ass. It will be the second dritch I have vanquished today."

The Interlocutor made a sort of low whistling sound, like someone burping into a clarinet. I think she was laughing.

"We are born to live in these border countries... Between these things called races, between these things called faiths, between these things called ideas, these things called worlds ... we are border creatures."

"So ... 'we' meaning you, and who else?"

"Even the Great Old Ones have their rules, a higher power to which they must answer."

As always, trying to get information out of the Interlocutor was like trying to read a book upside down. "You mean a government ... or a god?"

As I asked, I stared at the Interlocutor, fascinated. Flabby and smelling of burned chemicals, she no longer made me uneasy, even with those huge tentacles roiling and throbbing under her body, probing and seeking as if with a mind of their own. But the Interlocutor was looking at me keenly, with those gleaming, motionless eyes inside the torn mask of her face.

She looked me in the eye. "You have cultivated your garden," she said. "Been kind to what surfaces there..."

"Is this like, a metaphor?"

"...we are all border creatures, and if you live, and are not killed by the forces you oppose, and if you do not succumb, and join the forces of Yog-Sothoth, and this so-called Resurrection Church of the Ancient Gods – if none of this befalls you, Nate Silva, you may find that you are a border creature too."

I stood up, feeling a bit less achy and dizzy. "All I know is, we've got to get out of this stupid basement."

I stepped cautiously over to the stairs and mounted them to

check the steel door. I pounded on it and listened. Nothing. The door was heavy and solid and would not move, but there was that line of light around the edge: it had been put in hurriedly. The door was steel, but there might be weaknesses in the frame.

I went back down the stairs and moved around the floor. This part of the basement didn't occupy the huge space of the room above it. It was maybe ten metres by twenty. I found a padlocked steel door that felt rusty and dusty and, if anything, more impregnable than the door at the top of the stairs. I felt rough brick walls and then, raising my hands above my head, I felt a sheet of cardboard. I tore it off, showering my head with dirt, and saw a trickle of daylight through heavy steel mesh. When I'd been thrown down the stairs, I must have passed out, or maybe I'd fallen asleep before I started searching and found the Interlocutor. One way or another, hours had gone by. I pulled on the mesh, but everything in this old building was heavy duty. This was the stuff my dad's buddies used to bluster about: *Hamilton steel, made from the heart! The crap from China just ain't like how we useta make it!* I needed a tool: a pry bar or a hunk of pipe, or something, anything.

But the Church had gone through my pockets, and they wouldn't have thrown me down here unless they knew there was nothing here that would aid my escape. I continued to creep around the wall's perimeter. Against the opposite wall, the Interlocutor was silent; I was getting more and more worried about her. There was nothing I could do but keep trying to escape. The dirt floor was so rough; maybe if I groped around it would yield a good-sized brick or chunk of masonry.

I tripped, and fell into a hole.

"Jeez!" It was a deep hole too. I fell in up to my waist, and my feet were dangling into an abyss. I pulled myself out.

"What's this?" I cried out. "Hey, uh, Interlocutor ... there's a hole here. Maybe it's a tunnel." I turned around to see if I could see the hole in the dim light from the window. "A tunnel that leads ..."

"Every time the Church ... makes one of the ceremonies you call the midnight games ... contact is made ... something slips through."

"You mean, an invasive species?"

The Interlocutor took a deep breath. "All under the city there are such tunnels. In our tongue there is a word ... as they grow they become so deadly ... the word we use, *exanimator*..."

I reached out my hand, and felt something under it. Hard and flat and curved. I picked it up and shook it to see if it was strong enough to use as a pry bar. There was some kind of gunk on one end. As I tested it, I stepped forward and my foot struck a pile of such things.

"Aha," I announced. "Found something. They *did* leave something here, stupid Church losers. I will break us out of here." I went down on my knees, too distracted to pay attention to the Interlocutor. What were these things anyway? Some long and rounded, none of them evenly ground or lathed to smoothness, some big and heavy, some broken into bits. I felt a round one.

"Here's something," I said. "It feels like a five-pin bowling ball." I moved my hand and jerked backwards. I got up and tripped over something long and straight.

I felt it. A long wooden handle, ending in a rusted steel blade ...

"... which others call ... *dritch* ..." the Interlocutor continued.

I recognized this object, even though I couldn't see it. I'd held it in my hands many times before. At one end, a rusty blade; at the other end, near the tip, a rough spot that I always had to handle gingerly to avoid getting a splinter. It was unmistakably an object that had been pulled out of my hands just hours before. It was our garden hoe. With a shudder I stepped away from the hole I'd stumbled into, and from the pile of unfamiliar objects – on the round one I'd felt hair and eye sockets. I had been rooting around in a pile of human bones.

"I think I get the point."

I found the window and pried at the mesh with the blade of the hoe. Soon, I had raised a corner of it, and tried pulling with my hand, but the mesh was too strong. I kept at it until I had pulled out another of the spikes that bound it to the bricks, then another.

I poked the handle through the hole I'd made. It hit wood. I rammed at it, and the handle went through the thin, weather-beaten plywood that covered the window on the outside.

I peeked through the hole in the plywood, but the glimpse of sunlight was gone. Night had come again. Soon the final ceremony would begin.

Then I thought: the bottom stair had rattled when I leaned on it. I could see it now. I went and pried at one end. Rusted old spikes groaned and whined, and then one end came up. I pulled up the other end.

I hauled the timber to the top of the stairs and pounded it against the door. It didn't budge. I hauled back and pounded it into the edge of the door, and this time I heard the frame crack. Here's where I could make some progress. Mindful that this racket could attract the dritch back to us, wherever it was in the tunnels that supposedly criss-crossed the city, I did my best to hurry. The end of the timber was splintering; I pounded at the door frame, and the timber split in two. My hands slid along one half. The other half fell to the floor.

My hands were burning. I dropped the split timber and collapsed on the stairs.

"I'm making no headway," I announced to the Interlocutor. "I was almost there, but…"

The Interlocutor said nothing. I heard her take a deep breath, then her words came out slow and thick as glue. "I hear … the dritch is returning."

Cripes, I thought, some help here … please! But who am I going to find who can lend a hand with this, who?

"Well," I replied. "I guess we did our best. I just need to take a breath here, and I'll see if I can pry up another one of these steps. The last one filled my hand with splinters. But I almost got through. If I can make another try before the dritch …"

"Nate?" It was a familiar voice. "Nate, is that you? Is that you in there?"

I looked over my shoulder. There were shadows against the light of the door frame. I couldn't quite believe it. If anyone showed up, I figured it would be Church members, ready to finish us off if the dritch hadn't already got to us.

"Sam?" I asked.

"Nate?"

"Sam?"

"Nate?"

I heard another voice. "Enough, you guys. Look, we can unlatch this thing." I heard someone struggling with the deadbolt.

"Meghan?"

"Nate, we'll try to get you out. But the latch has been bent. Have you been pounding at the door?"

"A little bit."

"Nice job."

I heard another woman's voice. "Here, use the crowbar." Something cracked, and the door flew open.

I walked out, blinking into the light and saw Mehri. She was wearing old running shoes, blue jeans and a crappy-looking winter coat with fake fur around the hood. Now more than ever, she struck me as the best-looking human being ever created.

I blinked. "You look so great." Of course, right next to Mehri were Meghan and Sam.

"Uh, I mean all you guys," I added weakly. "It's great to see you." That was true, after all. They were all wearing functional-looking work clothes and lugging various tools: a crowbar, an axe, a sledgehammer.

"How did you know where to find me?"

"Duh," Sam said. "I looked out the window and saw you going down the railroad tracks? We all went to bed, but when your dad started phoning for you, we put two and two together."

"You've saved us," I said, "but we have to hurry."

"'Us'?" asked Sam.

I looked around. The place was a mess of homemade signs, spilled drinks, overturned chairs and, here and there, a few flowers from the flower stand, which still stood in front of the stage. I stepped past them and looked at the rubble.

"I just have to warn you," I said, "that not everyone involved in this … this whole thing with the Church … not everyone you're going to meet is, uh, exactly the kind of person you might expect, uh, to meet."

"What's what supposed to mean?" asked Sam. "Nate, are you feeling okay?"

"I'm great."

Actually, I felt rotten, but my main worry was the Interlocutor, who was getting weaker by the minute. As I talked, I found her scooter in the debris. I righted it, but it wouldn't power on. Various plastic tubes dripped fluids onto the cluttered floor.

"This belongs to the Interlocutor. Meghan, you know who she is. She's been beat-up by the Church's mob," I explained. "But she told me she has something … she's got, like, her own 911 …"

On the left-hand side of it, under the seat, I found the metal box that the Interlocutor had described. I found its protective panel and slid it to one side. There was a little plastic spoiler over a black button; I flipped it up and pressed the button.

"Ouch," I said. My hands were a mess. I pulled a black splinter from my right forefinger.

Meanwhile, nothing happened with the mechanism in front of me. No little light went on. I worried that the alarm depended on the chair's power system, which had been disabled. Then the chair spoke to me.

"Ensse … n'hraggi akh menganah … srrrubi …?"

I answered it. "The Interlocutor is injured and she needs help. We are at a place called the Resurrection Church of the Ancient Gods. It's an old warehouse at the end of Markle Avenue." I described how to get there – if they were driving, although for all I knew the Interlocutor's "team" would arrive by flying saucer.

"I think she needs help fast."

Meghan reached toward me. "Nate ... give me your hand."

I waved my hands impatiently. "We have to get the Interlocutor out of the basement." I had no idea if it would be any help, but I rolled the scooter to the basement door.

"You just have to know," I told them, "that the Interlocutor is not exactly a human being. She's from someplace else. But she is on our side and we have to help her." I had a thought. "What time is it anyway?"

I moaned when I got the answer: it was eight o'clock at night. I had wasted the whole day crawling around a warehouse basement.

Now I could at least see where I had been. Light flooded in from the open door, and my rescuers had a couple of flashlights. Against one wall I could see the gaping hole where the dritch had entered the day before, evidently bursting through to the main floor, surprising the Church members and causing mayhem. The pile of bones I'd been rooting through were scattered all over the cellar; earlier, when I'd been fumbling in the dark, I thought they were rocks or clods of earth. There were bones of all sizes. I glanced at the scene as I rushed to check on the Interlocutor.

She slumped against the brick wall, any luminosity either dimmed in the bright light, or faded altogether. Her tentacles shuddered as I touched her. They were still warm, but the T-shirt I'd tied around the one had turned black and shiny. Behind me, I heard Meghan gasp.

"What is that thing?"

"I just told you." I didn't want to complicate matters by explaining the new cosmogony (I was only just learning it myself) that included not only Earth and its multitude of species, but the Great Old Ones, the Hounds of Tindalos, the Interlocutor and, most urgently, the dritch.

"We have to get out of here," I said. "Come here and help me."

Nobody moved. I decided to phrase things differently. I did not want the dritch to ex-animate me. I felt barely animated as it was.

"Come here and help me right now," I repeated. "We have to get out of here." I turned to the Interlocutor. "Can you walk?"

I forced my arm under her upper arm. She gave a hoarse cry, and I felt her tentacles flex. Then Meghan appeared on the other side.

"It's so *big*," she said. We both heaved, and the Interlocutor's huge bulk wobbled up from the dirt floor, taking us with it. Together we staggered toward the stairs, flanked by Mehri and Sam as we made ridiculous sounds of encouragement: *here, almost there*, and when we reached the stairs, *now, up!* and then *keep going* until I smashed into the door frame. There wasn't room for all of us to go through. The Interlocutor, Meghan clinging to her side, collapsed onto what was left of her scooter. She turned her head toward me.

"Everything will happen soon," she said. "There will be no more contact between me and you."

"We've got to close that door," I said to Mehri and Sam, who were still keeping their distance.

Hardly taking their eyes off the Interlocutor, they helped swing the door shut. With the deadbolt thrown, it felt pretty secure, despite the mess I'd made of the frame.

"What the heck is a dritch?" Mehri asked.

"You must come," said the Interlocutor.

"We need to get out of here. If the Church people come back – and this Church has a lot of members – they'll throw us in that cellar, and the Interlocutor says the dritch is coming back."

"Come with me now," said the Interlocutor, "into the dark."

Meghan's eyes widened. "Oh my god."

The Interlocutor had extended her tentacles and was weakly trying to pull the scooter toward the front door, leaving smears of oily black ichor behind her. She had never looked more slimy and alien.

"It's okay," I told the others. "She needs our help."

"Nate," said the Interlocutor. "My departure ..."

"Here, wrap up your, uh, arms, and we'll ..." I turned to the others. "Help me. We've got to push her outside. Help is coming – for her anyway. But we *all* should get out anyway …"

There was a crash from the cellar, and we all jumped as something slammed into the door from the other side. There was the sound of rough, chitinous feelers probing the edge of the door, looking for a way out of the cellar and into the Church.

"Get out now," I said. "Hurry." As the others helped with the Interlocutor, I remembered where I'd heard my phone hit the wall. I searched around in the wreckage. There was my pocket knife; I scooped it up and kept looking.

Sam called, "Nate, didn't you say we should hurry?"

There it was! I pocketed my phone and caught up with Meghan, Mehri and Sam, who were gingerly guiding the Interlocutor out the front door. The scooter, warped and broken, barely rolled well enough to act as a rickety dolly. With a clatter of the crash bar, we pushed through the door into the Church's dark parking lot.

"Push me," the Interlocutor said. "The dark. This way." She gestured toward the far corner of the Church's compound. "You, Nate. Alone."

"It's easier if we all help."

She looked at the others and said to me, "It is not fair to bring your friends. They are not ready. Not everyone can live on the borders between worlds."

I wasn't sure what she meant, but if the dritch broke through the door – or went back through its tunnel and ambushed us in the dark – I wanted everyone out of here.

"She says you've got to go," I told the others. "Thank you. You saved us. But now, I need to take care of her. Someone is coming for her, and she says it's best if they're not seen. Get to the stadium. We've got to figure out something to disrupt the ceremony tonight. Anything."

It turned out they had all come in Meghan's car. "We've got some ideas," she said. "If we can get enough people together."

"You've got to be smart about it, Meghan. There's an awful lot of Church members. They're not afraid to hurt anyone who gets in their way. But if the ceremony tonight is a success ..." I didn't know how to describe to her the enormity of what that implied, so I wimped out. "Have you heard from Lovecraft?"

"Not a word," Meghan replied. "His so-called underground doesn't seem as if it does much. Frankly, we're talking about forming a group of our own," she told me excitedly. "I want to call it ..."

I shook my head. "Meghan. *GO*. Really."

We arranged to meet at the Shirazis' house, and I breathed a sigh of relief when Meghan started up her little Volkswagen and they drove off. I pushed the Interlocutor to the edge of the Church's freight yard. She peered around at the urban bushland, up at the sky and then she spoke. "There is something that must be seen."

CHAPTER 22
THE GHOST TRAIN

The night was clear, and looking back at the Church, I saw its ancient metal smokestacks outlined against the stars. I pushed the scooter, focusing on what the Interlocutor had just said. *What must be seen?* Despite her pain and weakness, she seemed to know exactly what she was doing. That was more than I could say for myself.

"Your friends," the Interlocutor said, "your friends call me *it*. To them, I am a *thing*."

"To be honest," I said wearily, "you take some getting used to." I decided to change the subject. "Where are we going? And when we were inside, how'd you know the dritch was approaching?"

"I hear," said the Interlocutor. "I want to get you into the dark." Before I could ask why, she unfurled a shuddering tentacle, pointing straight up, past the trees and the far-off glow of the city. "We come here so you can see. To show you this."

The sky was clear, splashed with glowing swirls and clouds and galaxies of stars as if some genius painter, turning in their sleep, had dreamed infinity, their brush filled with light.

"You are right, Nate," the Interlocutor said. "The forces we have are so small. You just have yourself, and your friends new and old, and me who is, as your friends say, only a *thing*. All around us, in this city alone, thousands are driven by want and greed and fear to grow up angry and predatory. They are feral, thinking only to use others for their own gain. From these, the Resurrection Church of the Ancient Gods has recruited its hungry many. Brought together by the Great Old Ones themselves, by the rulers of a planet that, through their science and formulae, they hope to intersect with yours.

"But they too are very small. Look how small they are, look, look. Even the Great Old Ones, who delight in twisting and deforming nature, fail to twist all species and all its creatures to their will. They have twisted humans to change the world, to make it more like their world, to warm the atmosphere and pollute the air and sea and soil, but still nature resists. Still living things find ways to live. Because your world itself is alive. It turns in the sun; and, like blood in a huge beating heart, its oceans throb and pulse to the sun on one side and the moon on the other; and it has seasons that make its atmosphere surge and bellow and blow from pole to pole and around its warm equator. It is a world full of pain and sweetness and death and great danger; the earth is a jewel in a universe of living things, and even as we run and hide and every second feel more desperate, there are forces working around us to disrupt the plans of the Great Old Ones, and to send them back to reform and revive their own world, the world they've spoiled."

"I wish they'd hurry up," I said.

"And look at your friends. I am saying that even though it seems as if you are feeling alone, you are not. Just think why they came here."

"It's a good thing they did, Interlocutor. They came here to save our butts."

"They did not come to save my butts. They came here to save your butts."

I didn't say a word. For starters, the Interlocutor had referred to being called a *thing*. It was my first taste of extraterrestrial sarcasm. I wondered if indeed it, or she, had feelings, and if we had hurt them.

The silence clung to us. Above us the stars hung so bright I could almost hear them hissing and sizzling, a million points of pure energy. And then I thought of something. But first the Interlocutor coughed wetly.

"And now I must go. They are coming for me," the Interlocutor wheezed. "I am shutting down."

"I just thought," I said, "there is another thing. Who is this sorcerer dude? I've heard the Church people talking about the sorcerer. They seem afraid of him, or her, whatever. Maybe if I can contact him, or her, this sorcerer person can help us. Wait a second – what did you just say?"

"They have hurt me, and I have been too long ... in this air. Too long – trying to intercede. It is time for me to go."

"You mean you're ... You're not *dying*, are you?"

"They are coming for me."

"Can I help you?" I touched the Interlocutor on her shoulder, or what passed for a shoulder underneath her ragged clothes. Through that greasy fabric I felt a pulse, struggling and slow, and the fading of that great internal heat.

"You should go," she said. "I have signalled them – the car, the am-bew-lance, it is coming for me. They don't want you ... people ... to see them ... they are not dangerous to you, but they are coming to help me. It is the way things are arranged."

Through the surrounding bush, I could hear the rattle of something big coming down the tracks. A glimmer of light outlined the smelly bulk of the Interlocutor hanging over her wrecked scooter.

"When will you be back?" As I spoke the Interlocutor stretched and I heard the ripping of fabric. Numberless tentacles, uncountable in the dark, flexed and extended, and I smelt dank alien smells of ammonia and rotten eggs.

"Go now – quickly." Sure enough, the flashing lights of the ambulance strobed through the trees around us, lights blotting out the stars. "I will tell you this ..."

I had turned to run, but as I looked back the Interlocutor shrank in her scooter, wrapping her tentacles around herself. "Sorcerer is not a person. Sorcerer, too, is a *thing*."

"You mean – look, I'm sorry you got called that. It's just – all this is new to us, and I never knew anything, I mean anyone, like you existed, but you've been a big, uh, support ..."

"... not a *thing* like me." The Interlocutor buried her head in her rubbery arms, and shrank in her seat like a flower retreating before the night. She let out a weak cry, and her tentacles, wrapped around her, flexed and convulsed like firehoses.

The Interlocutor looked at me dully. Her voice was a harsh whisper. "Go."

She closed her eyes, and suddenly her body came loose in its seat and she leaned forward over the broken controls and was still. The wind was rising again, and above me clouds were shutting out the stars. Suddenly what she had called an "am-bew-lance" loomed out of the dark. It was huge and black, and it rolled down the train tracks with the rumble of well-greased wheels. I pulled the Interlocutor back from the fence as the locked gates were torn off their hinges and fell aside, and the rail car crashed into the neglected freight yard that the Church had taken over. It seemed that the Interlocutor's panic button had worked. I felt a surge of relief.

"They're here," I said. "They'll help."

I put my hand on her shoulder but she did not move or speak. The heat was fading from the oily bulk under my fingers, and I realized her rescuers, if they were coming to save her, had come too late.

I turned and, as fast as I could, jumped the chain at the road entrance, which hurt me all over, and pushed my way into the trees and back onto the tracks, then out toward the lights of the city. I looked back; light flooded from the ghost train. From a sliding door in the side, silhouettes (human, as far as I could see) were lowering a sling of some kind. I heard a man's voice: "She's dead!" Suddenly I was blinded by a spotlight from the black boxcar. "What'd you do to her, you son of a bitch?"

I ducked into the bushes until I came to a curve in the tracks, then I ran until I reached Barton. I headed down the street, away from the train tracks and this mystery boxcar and its mystery destination.

My phone buzzed. Without looking I put it to my ear, expecting to hear my father.

"Dad?"

"Nate! Where in the world have you been? Your father ..."

"Mr. Lovecraft ... Howard ... I'm coming from the Resurrection Church. I had a plan ... but it didn't work out ... so I tried to help the Interlocutor. That didn't work out, either. Are you and Dad working on that barrel?"

"It has been finished," Lovecraft announced proudly. "Every angle rounded off. Meanwhile, your father has gone out, I know not where."

Without going into every detail of what had happened since last night, I confessed to Lovecraft that I had attempted to steal the parchment back from my father and pass it to the Proprietor, but that, evidently, I had failed.

"I beg your forgiveness, Nate," he replied. "I was complicit in that deception. Your father was afraid you would try such a thing. Before we retired for the night, I helped him make a counterfeit that you would easily find."

I felt a surge of anger. "Aren't you guys smart."

"We were afraid you might try to take things into your own hands ..."

It would have worked. Lovecraft kept talking.

"I am in the process of mustering reinforcements. If the ceremony ..."

"I've lost this whole day," I said, "locked in a goddamn basement. Somebody's got to help my father."

"If they get here in time, this can be turned around."

"If if if," I said through clenched teeth.

I ended the call and sighed, and looked ahead down the dark corridor of the train tracks. Out there they were assembling: The Resurrection Church of the Ancient Gods, their legion of followers, the Great Old Ones, the Hounds of Tindalos. If Dad and Lovecraft dropped the ball, my father would die.

I started running. As I put distance between myself and the Resurrection Church, I slowed down, out of breath. All around me the stars were vanishing, the darkness thickening as clouds blew across the moon, and street lights flickered, rocked by a rising wind. I ran across Gage, past the FreshCo, so as to stay off the street where I could be spotted, through the big parking lot that was always empty except for idling semis or cops on their break. But tonight the lot was filling up. Cars came out of the darkness and out of them swarmed excited families, who headed across Barton and down the side streets toward Ivor Wynne. The crowds shrieked as the wind rose; I felt a slap of rain and zipped up my hoodie. The air around me thundered, as if the Great Old Ones themselves had burst from the crumbling walls of their adopted church and were whirling through the streets toward their coronation.

The sky opened up in a cloudburst, and I threw myself against the cinder-block wall of the neighbourhood car wash. As lightning lit the sky, I looked up at the golden domes of St. Vladimir, and the clouds seemed to flex and grimace into living shapes with the excitement of the approaching ceremony.

Then I remembered what Lovecraft had just said. Everything was going great, except that "your father has gone out, I know not where."

Why would Dad go out, as the Hounds drew near, when he and Lovecraft had just finished the enclosure that would keep him safe? I remembered what Dad had said the other day, when I'd walked him to the bus: "I can't have that goddamn Church taking everyone away from me."

Then I realized exactly what Dad had in mind. Suddenly I did something I hadn't done since I was a little boy. Without thinking or planning or believing that anyone was listening, I started to pray.

"Just let my dad get out of this," I said. "Don't let him get killed by these bastards from the Church, or by Yog-Sothoth, or get fed to a dritch, or torn apart by the Hounds. Just keep him safe. To me, you can do anything you want. Just give me this."

I squinted against the glare as three bolts of lightning struck – first the rusted smokestacks that were now the Resurrection

Church, then the suns and crosses atop St. Vladimir, then the distant light towers of the football stadium – all the frail and fragmentary shields we put up against the hissing immensities beyond us, the light years of space and the indifferent, unstoppable millennia that were converging tonight, all our hopes that, for one brief instant, they might shed a single tear for the human race. I ran out into the rain and as the storm raged, I kept running.

PART 3
THE LEAGUE OF UNMARRIED GENTLEMEN

She bent her head, thinking. "The serpent is a sorcerer. We must find a sorcerer to tell us what is the danger."

    – Brian Moore, *Black Robe*

CHAPTER 23
DOOMED

The rain stopped by the time I reached the stadium, but black clouds loomed as if a mountain range had magically risen over the city. I avoided the growing crowd as much as I could. If someone spotted me, I didn't want to be surrounded. Some of these people had been at the Church the night before, and could recognize me as the troublemaker who should have been gobbled up hours ago.

"We are here!" some guy shouted from the front entrance. "Come one, come all!"

My plan was to skirt the edges of the crowd, wait until a group surged through the front entrance, then join the surge and exit the crowd as soon as I got inside the gates. But as I drew closer I saw Clare at the entrance. She would spot me for sure. I moved along until I saw Kara with a group of friends at the next entrance. This was also too big a risk.

I jogged around to the south end and, sure enough, there was no one around that shadowy corner that Dana had showed me. His silver-painted zip ties were still in place. I sawed at them with the tiny blade of my pocket knife, glad I'd picked it out of the rubble at the Church, until one by one they gave way. I slipped through the gap in the fence.

There was no one in this part of the stadium yet. The feeling was very different from the previous game. At the snack bar, the friendly bartender from the other night was idly thumbing his smartphone, its frigid glow the only light for several metres around. I made my way to an entrance to the bleachers.

A tent set up on the field was lit by propane lamps, its translucent sides strobing and flickering with the excited shadows of the cult members within. A cheer went up from the bleachers: the gates had opened and the lower tiers were already filling up; followers were taking their places for the ceremony to come. *We are all here* – the words echoed and whispered through the crowd, until someone shouted it from high in the stands: "We are all here." Tonight their lives, all of our lives, would change. It would be a new world.

All I could think was, I've got to find Dad. I ran into the nearest stairway, scanning the face of everyone I could see. Eleven p.m. was not far off.

I could see the Proprietor going in and out of the tent, and Clare and Jimmy were there too. Nobody was looking my way. In the distance, at the far edge of the stadium, I heard someone shout, "We are all here," and at that second I felt that pulse in the air, that oscillating sound that made the darkness above the stadium into a living thing, like an engine of destiny and menace and malice.

My phone buzzed in my pocket, and I snatched it up without looking at the display.

"Nate." Lovecraft sounded out of breath. "My friends have arrived, and we've transported the prepared storage drum to the stadium."

"Is this because you think Dad has gone to the stadium, intending to bring the Hounds of Tindalos down upon the heads of the Resurrection Church, even if it means his own death?"

"Well …"

"Where are you, Howard?" I asked. "You've got to tell me where you are."

"In the first place, Nate, we can't have you coming to the stadium. It's just too dangerous. If –"

"I'm already inside the stadium. If you'll tell me where you and the drum are, I will find my father and bring him to you."

"How on earth will you do that?"

"*Howard, please tell me where you are.*"

"Why, we're parked just outside the front entrance – just at the edge of this massive crowd that's –"

I hung up, looked at the time again and ran out into the playing field.

I couldn't see my father anywhere, and I hoped against hope that he had changed his mind and was seeking Lovecraft out at this very moment. Or that he had found someplace where he would be safe; someplace that was all curves and liquid and whispering leaves and soft angles; the safe place that Evelyn Dick's husband had sought at Albion Falls, and failed to find.

Then I saw his face in the dim periphery of the light from the tent. He was watching it, waiting, glancing at his wristwatch. He was not glad to see me, and pulled me back into the shadows so we wouldn't be noticed.

"Goddammit, kid." He had to shout to be heard over the noise of the growing crowd. "Get out of here."

"Dad, listen to me. Lovecraft is here. He and his buddies from the Underground have brought the storage drum. All the angles have been smoothed out of it. You can go and get inside – right now."

He pointed toward the tent. "We're just a few yards away from that bastard and his toadies. At the stroke of eleven I'll run in there. If these so-called Hounds truly do appear, we'll let the chips fall where they may."

"Believe me, Dad," I pleaded. "They appear. They truly do. You'll get killed."

"Maybe, maybe not. The main thing is, the SOBs who run this show will be right in the middle of it. This has to stop – once and for all."

"But you'll be dead."

"Maybe they'll take out some Church members as well as me. The main thing is, nobody will want to go near the Resurrection Church ever again."

"But you'll be dead. I'll be an orphan."

He shrugged. "You can always go live with your Uncle Don."

"Have you lost your mind?" I gestured at the crowd around us. "You haven't seen what the Hounds do to people. They ripped

Dana's head off. What will they do if you let them loose in a crowd? I know these people have been suckered in by a bad cause, but does that mean they should die? That you need to die?"

Dad sighed and looked at his watch. "Christ," he said, "we're running out of time. Where do I go?"

The crowd was swelling in size; there were easily twice as many people as at the last ceremony. By now, all pretense of crowd control had been shattered. The gates to the stadium had been thrown open, and Dad and I pushed our way through the excited horde as I led him out into the street.

A little ways down the block, a small group clustered around an old pickup truck with Pennsylvania licence plates. In the back, lying on its side was the storage drum from our basement.

"Besides," I admitted, "I can't stand Uncle Don."

"Nate, Gordon, thank goodness you're here," Lovecraft said excitedly. He introduced us to a petite woman in her forties, her long black hair streaked with grey. "Agnes feels our chances for success are excellent."

"This is nothing," Agnes said matter-of-factly. "When the Resurrection Church of the Ancient Gods set itself up in Ciudad Juárez in 1993, they achieved great power in a very short period of time. In fact, they might have made the breakthrough if not for three factors: a rebellion, led by workers from the maquiladoras, that disrupted the penultimate ceremony; an attack on the Church executives by the Hounds themselves, who had been summoned so often that they had found ways to circumvent the control of the Church; and the protection of the rebellion's leader from a casting of the runes. Her friends had improvised a defence quite like this one. She concealed herself in it and, at the appointed time, in a cloud of blue smoke, the Hounds disappeared as fast as they appeared. Moments later, she emerged safely."

"Agnes is being too modest," Lovecraft said. "*She* was the leader of the rebellion. If the Church had their way, she wouldn't be gracing us –"

"Howard," blushed Agnes. She rolled her eyes. "As usual, you are too kind." She held up two fingers. "I was this close to the so-called god Yog-Sothoth, and I witnessed the sorcerer's emergence from the world of the Great Old Ones, R'lyhnygoth, into our world."

"Ah," I said. "The sorcerer. So, just who is …?"

"But we beat them back." Agnes turned back to the truck. "And now," she continued, "we have to get this man into the disangled sanctuary; there isn't much time. So, Howard, you're confident that you've rounded off every angle?"

Lovecraft nodded. "It's a small space, and I worked on it carefully all morning." The driver got out of the pickup and lowered the tailgate.

"I hope everything's okay in there," he said. "The suspension on this old beater ain't what it useta be, and some of the potholes in this town …" He shook his head. Another man began to unclamp the lid of the drum.

I looked at my phone. The hour was near, for sure. If everything went okay, I would ask Agnes later about the sorcerer. "Thanks for doing this," I said to Dad.

He shrugged. "Thanks for coming to get me, kid."

"I don't know what we're going to do," I said, "but I know we can do something, without you going and sacrificing yourself."

Actually, that wasn't completely true. I had no idea how to go about disrupting tonight's ceremony, with so many people here to beckon and buttress Yog-Sothoth. I was playing this by ear, hoping someone else could come up with an idea.

The lid of the drum was removed. "Damn," I heard the driver say, softly. "Like I said, those potholes …"

Crumbling plaster spilled out into the truck bed. The inside of the drum was filled with it. The gentle curves that Lovecraft had laboured over were all gone, and the barrel was filled with rubble.

"Agnes, Howard," I said, "You guys are the experts. There must be something we can do. Dad …"

I looked around. My father was gone.

CHAPTER 24
THE HOUNDS

As I entered the playing field a figure loomed over me. A dark-bearded man with a long curved apparatus slung around his neck, his features concealed by a hooded sweatshirt.

"What are you doing here?"

I saw Meghan and the others threading toward us through the growing crowd. "Mr. Shirazi," I said, "I'm trying to find my father."

"Go home," he said. "My group is here as well, along with members of the Lovecraft Underground. Tonight, the evil one will not get through. But it's dangerous. Go home – go to my house. Play video games with Sam."

"I can't do that, Mr. Shirazi." I gestured and he turned. Sam was standing behind him, with Mehri and his other sisters. While Mr. Shirazi let his offspring know that he was not pleased, Meghan approached me, but I shook my head.

"There's no time," I said. "I have to find my dad." I tore away from them and made my way through the crowd.

Ahead of me I heard a man shout, but he wasn't shouting, "WE ARE ALL HERE." It was my father's voice, and the crowd parted around him as he held the flickering shapes of the runes over his head, the parchment he had tricked me into giving to him, then replaced with a counterfeit to prevent me from stealing it back.

"Hey, you bastards," he yelled. "When you targeted my boy, you messed with the wrong dude. Well, in about –" he checked his watch again "– sixty seconds, you'll get a chance to see how badass you really are, you so-called Resurrection ..."

I heard the Proprietor's voice. I started toward the tent.

"What the hell is he doing here?" the Proprietor shouted. "Stop him. That's the only way to protect us from the Hounds. You know what I mean."

I totally understood what he meant. The Hounds would not come if their victim was dead.

Jimmy and two other men erupted from the tent and headed in different directions into the crowd. They were carrying baseball bats.

My father saw them coming and started weaving through the crowd, getting closer to the tent while keeping as many bodies as he could between him and his pursuers. When I was fifteen metres away, our eyes met. He stopped. The roaring in the sky above grew louder. A blue mist began to rise from the damp grass of the stadium. Around me the shadows moved, as if to dodge the rising of an alien sun.

"Nate," Dad yelled, as Clare appeared from the crowd and grabbed his shoulder. He twisted away and ran, gesturing at me to get away. "Far away!"

I blinked, unable to believe what I was seeing. The blue mist, circling my father's knees, turned into a spiral of blue smoke that whirled around us, edged in blackness. A void dropped out of the air: a gateway into space-time unimaginably dark and remote. Against that darkness glimmered a whiteness of bone as two fleshless paws emerged, then a blind savage head with teeth like razors, sniffing and seeking this way and that, this way and that, and I shuddered from my head to my toes and prayed that it didn't catch my scent. Slouching into the cold autumn air – followed by another and another and another – the Hounds of Tindalos emerged onto the field.

"RUN," my father shouted.

And then the Hounds were upon him. The crowd around my father exploded in every direction, leaving Dad alone on the turf, grasping the parchment. Seeing he only had seconds to act, he ran toward the tent. The hound nearest to me turned to follow him.

Each hound was an intricate jigsaw puzzle of tiny, glowing bones, joined at a thousand sharp angles, and each joint crackled and sparked as it moved sinuously across the dark field.

Jimmy was in the crowd beside me, frozen in his tracks with his mouth wide open. He dropped his baseball bat and started fumbling at his pants pockets. I threw myself in front of him, grabbed up the bat and ran after the hound. I smashed at its rear haunch, thinking – I guess – to distract it from my dad.

The hound stopped, and with both hands around the bat I smashed it again. Really hard this time.

It turned. I might as well have been hammering at the side of a bulldozer. As I jumped out of its way, the hot blast of its talons ripped through my shirt and knocked me to the ground. I rolled to the side and tried to squirm away but the hound pinned my legs and raised its forepaw to strike again. Then it shrieked ... and shrieked again, and turned to defend itself as something struck it from behind.

"You will go hungry tonight," a man shouted. In the smoke I saw Mr. Shirazi, his glasses reflecting the snaps of lightning from the roaring sky. He drew back from the hound and raised the Delphic scythe. Its glowing hook struck a burst of sparks from the creature as Mr. Shirazi deflected its pounce with the blade. He struck again, and the hound roared in pain and then the sound died as its snout, and then its talons, and then its chest and haunches and the rest of its body, burst into sparks. The hound's body shuddered, sparks sizzling between its fiery joints and angles, and in a rolling stink of charcoal and sulphur it burst apart and was gone, leaving behind the smell of apocalypse. I fell back onto the cold grass.

Mr. Shirazi bent over me. "Nate? Are you all right?"

"You killed that thing ..." I let him help me up. "Where can I get one of those?" I faced him straight on so that he couldn't see that my tattered shirt was wet with blood.

"Head for the stands," he said. "Hide. Stay out of the way." He looked up. "Help him," he said to someone behind me.

Lovecraft was standing over me. "We've got to get to the public address system," he said. "I need your help."

"Howard, do you think it's over? Look what Mr. Shirazi just did." I tried to ignore the pain. With luck, all this would be over very soon. "Where's my dad?"

"The forces unleashed by the Hounds are making this threshold the strongest one so far. If the ceremony continues, things will only get worse. For one thing, every exanimator in the area will be drawn to –" he gasped. "Nate, you're bleeding."

"What about my father?"

A loud cracking sound came from the crowd, not far from us. Mr. Shirazi swore in Persian. "Some idiot is shooting off a gun," he shouted. "Stay down." And he was gone in the crowd.

"We can't stay here. We've got to get off the ground," Lovecraft said. Across the field, another man with a scythe had surprised a hound, and with mechanical shrieks like torn metalwork, like fireworks in reverse its tracery of light shrank and collapsed into a plume of blue smoke. Everywhere in the chaos I could hear screams, voices calling for loved ones, children calling for their parents. I heard the popping of gunshots. The police had shown up from somewhere. Near the tent, a constable fired several shots into a hound; it turned and was on him in a second. I tore my eyes away, searching for my father.

I pushed away from Lovecraft and weaved through the panicking crowd. I saw a shadow at the end of the field; a man in a dark business suit, running for cover at one of the stadium entrances. It was the Proprietor. Then I stumbled over something soft. I looked down at the body of a Hamilton city cop. In the flashing lights and smoke, I could see he had no head. Numbly I looked around for it, as if reconnecting this poor dude's head with his corpse would make things better. And there, a metre or so beyond his outstretched hand, I saw the gun.

It was whatever sidearm the police use; a flat automatic pistol of some kind, lying there on the grass like a hunk of obsolete computer hardware. When I bent over to pick it up, the slashes from the hound's talons pulled open and I felt blood trickling down. That was okay; it didn't feel very serious and I was sure I had lots of blood to spare. I hefted the gun in my hand; it was heavy. I ignored the sound of Lovecraft calling me, and took off after the Proprietor.

CHAPTER 25
SORCERER

It was dark inside the stadium doorway, and I thought of all the things that might be in that darkness: maybe a dritch had dug its way up from the sewers; or a hound (they would have a hard time hiding in the dark, unless they could turn off the horrible internal burning of their glowing bones); or some darker and nastier version of the Interlocutor, tentacled and hungry, a border creature who had chosen the dark side. But of all those monsters, worst of all was the Proprietor himself: a waxy, control-hungry prick who, so long as he got power and money and influence for himself and his buds, didn't care what happened to the planet and the rest of us living here.

"Only in the movies do handguns solve problems," Dad used to tell me. "In real life, they just make problems worse." True as this might be, with nothing around me making any sense, I could only think of how much damage and misery the Proprietor caused – with his tricks and his lies and his cult and his midnight games. He was ready to sell out the whole planet, starting with those he considered least important, people like Dana, using them as stepping stones to more and more power, to trample everyone for his own gain, even if it meant being a king in a ruined world. In fact, he should be ashamed to be alive, I thought. Getting rid of him would be a win-win situation. I confess that I was not at my most lucid. I was soaked in blood, it hurt to move and I was feeling kind of nauseous.

I stumbled into a wall and then found the stairs and made my way up to the bleachers. I scanned them up to the top, shadows dancing in the flashes of light from the commotion on the field. A wind was rising, and the clouds over the stadium whirled and glowed. Above the sounds of suffering and chaos below, I heard the subdued roar of the sky, the same roar I had heard at the previous games when, for me at least, this had all begun. One of the shadows zoomed into focus – it was the Proprietor. He was moving upward through the bleachers, approaching the rim of the stadium, arguing and pleading with someone over a cellphone pressed to his ear.

I started up toward him, treading those worn steps as Dana and I had – it seemed like years ago. I ducked into the seats when the Proprietor turned around, and then started up again. I was gaining on him. In any case, there wasn't much farther up he could go.

The roaring of the sky was gaining in intensity and somehow, crazily down on the field, I felt that the ceremony – despite the police, despite the Hounds, despite Mr. Shirazi and his Delphic scythe – was carrying on. One by one the Hounds were dispersing and vanishing, and a chant was rising from the ragged crowd that had gathered. There was the same change in the light, the same charged feeling in the air as the roaring mounted, although this time the wind was rising, as if the eye of a tornado had centred on Ivor Wynne Stadium and a funnelling whirlwind, expanding outward from that centre of greed and desire, was growing to engulf us all. A voice came over the sound system: "Cthulhu is near! Have faith in him and in me! Tonight is the night!"

It was the voice of the Proprietor – relayed somehow through his cellphone. I could see him mouthing the words as he stood at the rim of the stadium, his normally waxy hairdo spun into wavelets by the winds, fighting for balance as he rallied for this one last chance to carry out the bidding of the Great Old Ones he served. He hadn't noticed me yet. I shouted an insult, but it was carried away by the storm.

"Proprietor!" I called again, and raised the handgun, intending, even at this distance and in this storm, to fire and keep firing until the bastard went down. I aimed, lining up the sight of the barrel with his dark figure, and pulled the trigger.

Nothing happened. It was jammed or something. I looked at it, but suddenly was caught in a gust of wind so strong that the gun was almost blown right out of my hand. The roaring of the winds grew and engulfed me. I stumbled, tried to right myself against a seat, but a powerful gust blew me into the stands. And Lovecraft finally caught up with me.

"Nate – put that down."

A blaze of light exploded as something enormous appeared at the stadium's rim – the grey horizon of the city ripped open to reveal a vast blackness, and, as the winds grew, I smelled the smell of death and decay and burning. I ducked as something flew toward me, something alive, bat-like and chittering, with flashing teeth and great black eyes and leathery wings. The storm before me turned hot. Twigs and vegetation blew through this hole in the night, and something enormous began to take shape in the void that had opened above the stadium: a writhing mass that filled the night sky. It was alive, it moved and groped like a huge animal, but light shone from within it. When it made a sudden move, the light surged unbearably, and I closed my eyes and saw an afterimage of countless tentacles, covered in huge glowing suckers like globes of light, a network of flesh and fibres and unnameable angles that were this thing's veins and capillaries and nerves. The air shuddered, and suddenly underneath me the stadium buckled, and I heard the cracking of concrete, and the Proprietor's voice.

"The great god has come! He brings a new age! He brings new hope! He brings new wisdom! Let us praise him, Yog-Sothoth, Yog-Sothoth knows the gate. Yog-Sothoth is the gate. Yog-Sothoth is the key and guardian of the gate. Past, present, future, all are one in Yog-Sothoth. He knows where the Great Old Ones broke through of old, and where They shall break through again. He knows where They have trod earth's fields, and where They still tread them, and why no one can behold Them as They tread. *Y'AI'NG'NGAH / YOG-SOTHOTH!*"

An opening yawned among the writhing shapes in the sky, and Yog-Sothoth's voice sounded like a thousand truck horns. It was a clarion call of victory and I thought for a second maybe I should just stand back here – maybe there *IS* a new boss in town! Then I remembered why I was there. I raised the pistol, but Lovecraft smashed it out of my hand and it clattered off among the benches.

"Nate!" shouted Lovecraft. "Have you gone out of your mind?"

I stared at the creature that was pulling itself out of a gap in space onto the rim of Ivor Wynne Stadium. One of Yog-Sothoth's tentacles brushed against a light tower. The steel tower broke off like a twig, shattered on the bleachers and fragments sprayed onto the field. The cry of the Great Old One rattled through my skeleton, but then there was another blast of light, and the unearthly trumpet sound dropped a tone or two, as if as if the winds of victory had suddenly shifted.

I heard new screams from the crowd in the field below. The last of the hounds was running – fleeing – and suddenly it was seized by an enormous black shape that struck at it like a cobra, raised it in its mandibles high into the night sky, and swallowed it like a python sucking down a rat. In the flickering lights of the tent I saw that it was an enormous dritch – far larger than the one I'd battled in my backyard. Then the lamps in the tent guttered and went dark, as the tent itself lurched sideways and dropped into an enormous sinkhole that split the middle of the field. Out of the growing chasm emerged more of the creatures, of different sizes – I counted three, then seven, pounding up out of the dark. Each and every one of them was heading up the bleachers toward the growing continuum threshold – heading for exactly where Lovecraft and I were standing.

Lovecraft grabbed my arm. "Why did you take my gun?" I demanded.

"Exanimators," he said. "If we can conceal ourselves, they'll pass us by. They have sensed the energy field of the continuum threshold, and their instincts beckon them to return to their home world."

A gout of blue flame shot out of the opening in the sky, and now it was unmistakeable: Yog-Sothoth's bellow had become a scream of agony. Suddenly the Proprietor's voice, coming over the sound system, was drowned out by a voice that came from both the sky above and from inside my skull, a grinding bass rumble that trembled the air as it rose to a shriek.

"*Father!* Why do you let them hurt me – *Father?*"

"My god." Beside me, Lovecraft stopped in his tracks, looking up at Yog-Sothoth. He turned and looked at me, his mouth hanging open, his eyes welling with tears. "Did you hear that?" he sobbed.

"You've got to fight the voice, Howard."

"It is worse than I dreaded. I'm sorry, Nate. I've got to get away from here. Far away. Tell everyone, I'm sorry."

He tore himself away and ran down a few steps. Then he stopped and turned.

"Whether the battle is lost, or won!" he cried. He turned and ran. I called out a warning to him as I saw the long brittle legs of a dritch, its black bulk pulling itself up into the bleachers. Lovecraft swerved to avoid it, but the dritch ignored him and kept coming up. Now the Proprietor was the one in its path.

"Don't take me! Take him!" The Proprietor rose up to his full height. He was attempting to command the dritch. As it passed me, it turned. This wasn't one of the bigger dritches that had emerged from the field and now were scuttling up the bleachers to the continuum threshold. It turned toward me, feelers rattling in the night air, until its mandibles hung inches from my face. I backed up a few steps.

"Kill him!" the Proprietor shouted.

I reached out and brushed my hand against one of the boney feelers that ringed the dritch's monstrous head.

"Is that you?" I asked. "Stumpy?"

With an exasperated *whoosh*, the dritch blew air out of the circle of holes that lined its serpent-like abdomen. Then shuddering and clacking, it pivoted away from me and headed to the stadium's edge.

Above us, another enormous shape filled the opening, and as I beheld it, the opening itself started to shrink and weaken, the edges of the night sky scorched like burning paper, and Yog-Sothoth pulled itself back from the stadium's edge. Something else, just as huge, was pushing its way through the dimensional breach, but it was not an Ancient God. Perhaps it was another of the Great Old Ones, but whatever it was, it was ringed with fire – was there some war in this infernal heaven, that the Great Old Ones were now bringing to earth?

Seeing that I remained uneaten, the Proprietor turned and raised his arms against the wind, in supplication to his ancient god.

"Almighty Yog-Sothoth," he shouted, "cast the hands of foulness from our throats! *Iä! Shub-Niggurath!* You who are the gateway, let the great sphere meet, enter and save –" The Proprietor threw himself prone at the stadium's edge, as something huge emerged, flying low; part of it clipped the stadium's top as it crossed from R'lyhnygoth into our world, bringing with it a wind that pounded like a hurricane.

Unable to stand against the gale, I fell to my knees and wrapped my arms around a bench so I wouldn't be blown away. I looked up to see this monstrous thing. It was not a god or monster or alien, it was an enormous dirigible, passing mere metres over the top of the stadium, close enough for me to see the ancient, flaking fabric of its huge bulk. It was as if one of the mountain-sized freighters, built to haul tonnes of steel halfway across the world, had taken to the air.

Squinting against the wind, I gasped as the acreage of its rubbery sides passed over me, showing me a string of incomprehensible characters – R102 G-FAAX – and then a glowing line of windows, amazed faces pressed against the glass, shooting past in a blur, and then the source of the roar that had hovered over the stadium on these accursed nights: engines the size of freight cars, sparking and spinning and humming a tone so low that my bones vibrated along with the seats beside me and the cement steps I sprawled over. It soared over the stadium, and then flickered into transparency; suddenly, through it I saw the glow of the horizon, and then as fast as it had entered the night sky, it was gone again. The roar of its engines lingered then faded, echoing over the industrial fields to the north. I blinked dumbly, shocked at its sudden appearance and disappearance, and saw once more in my mind's eye the vessel's name, in fading and flaking paint, but still vast and imperious across the airship's bulk, in letters four metres high: *SORCERER.*

CHAPTER 26
AFTERMATH

With the passage of the airship, the smoke of the Hounds' appearance had been scoured from the air, and as the wind died down, once more the stadium was lit by little more than the glow of the city night. The swarm of dritches had passed, happily wiggling their huge carcasses back through the continuum threshold to their home world. At least *they* had had a good night.

I pushed myself to my feet and started down the stairs. All over the field people ran, some still trying to escape, some calling for help, some stooped over motionless bodies, and parts of bodies. There were wails of agony and grief, and a rising chorus of approaching sirens. No one paid me any notice as I reached the ground level and searched for Dad among the dead and the living, avoiding the gaping pits and the mounds of soil from the surfacing dritches.

"Dad!" I called, and when no one answered, "Gord! Gordon Silva!"

Still no one answered. I knew my dad was gone, and that no one else would answer me. I was just a kid who couldn't do anything, didn't know anything, would only get in the way. Across the field I saw the lights of emergency vehicles. Thinking of myself as a full-fledged orphan, I shivered as a breeze rose in the wake of the intersecting worlds, shivered because the front of my hoodie was soaking wet.

I stepped on something and stumbled as it rolled away. Dammit, I thought, more bones, bare bones. Then I fell onto all fours and looked at the thing up close: a baseball bat with a shattered handle, its unravelling tape dark with blood. My vision blurred and I shook my head until it hurt, and tried to find the strength to stand up. But maybe because of the continuum threshold, I was having a problem with gravity: my body had become unaccountably heavy. Just wait a minute, I thought, just a minute, and your strength will return. I sank onto my face on the cold grass, and lay there having thoughts about strength. If you rest long enough, it comes back. Suddenly, a man put his hand on my neck.

"This one's alive," he said, but I was busy having thoughts. I thought about the airship that had passed over, how that thundering during the midnight games was not the rumbling of doom, but the engine noise from the *Sorcerer*. A vessel that had been trying to get home for a long time.

"What's your name, son?" My face was getting lightly slapped. An antique dirigible, that had gone farther and longer than any ship ever invented.

"Hey, kid, stay with us. Can you say your name?"

I knew that my father was dead, and that even though the ceremony had failed, the church had been defeated, and the will of Yog-Sothoth had been broken, my own little world had been destroyed, bent beyond recognition, changed forever.

I blinked wearily, and I told them everything I could.

CHAPTER 27
THE SURVIVORS

Meghan, as far as I could tell, was never more in her element than when she was letting people know how stupid they were.

"For your information," she crisply told the nurse, "his name is not Sorcerer. That's not even his nickname. What kind of a name is that?" She told the nurse my particulars, as far as she knew them.

The nurse looked at the chart. "The paramedics asked him, and that's what he said."

Meghan looked at me and furrowed her eyebrows. "He was delirious. The poor little guy was in pain."

The nurse shrugged. "It says that exsanguination was a definite concern."

The "poor little guy" comment didn't bother me. My chest and shoulder, raked by the hound's talons, weren't bothering me much either. I felt no compulsion to open my eyes. I could lie there forever if they let me. I kept listening, and eventually I realized that Meghan and the nurse were gone.

The next day I had a short visit with a youngish French-Canadian guy, Dr. Martin. "Slight concussion," he said. That had happened in the church at the end of Markle Avenue. "Miscellaneous cuts and contusions. It's these lesions on the chest and shoulder that I don't get."

"Lesions?" I asked. "They're scratches."

Dr. Martin chuckled. "They are some serious scratches. They'll leave scars, but the actual wounds are healing well. There was no infection, because the wounds were so clean. How did you say you got them?"

"Claws."

He smiled. "Nate, I've heard your story about these so-called hounds. Do you know why I know these wounds weren't caused by an animal?"

"They *were* caused by an animal."

"Because, like I said, some of the flesh at the edges was blistered. No animal's claws would leave cuts like that. Whatever made these lesions was intensely hot. Even where it ripped through your clothes, the fabric was singed and blackened."

"The Hounds of Tindalos," I said, "are animals from another dimension, that evolved in angled space, as opposed to curved. We call them Hounds, but they're not canines, if you know what I mean. They're not like regular hounds."

"So, they are hounds made out of, let's say ... molten lava?"

I'm sure that Dr. Martin – "hey, man, call me Derek" – was using a patronizing tone at this point, but somehow it didn't bother me a bit. In fact, I laughed.

"It's not that simple, Derek, but you're getting warm. Hey, I made a joke: getting warm, get it?"

Dr. Martin looked at his watch. "Nate, I've got to move on. Much as I'm enjoying this talk."

"Me too." I grinned. "I'm *really* enjoying it."

"That'll be the painkillers." He patted my shoulder, making me wince (the painkillers weren't one hundred per cent), and left.

UNFORTUNATELY (it seemed at the time), they steadily reduced my dosage, so in a couple of days I was in better health, but enjoying myself less. Meghan did nothing to boost my self-esteem when I told her how I'd picked up the policeman's sidearm and tried, and failed, to shoot the Proprietor.

"What a stupid thing to do."

So far in the hospital I'd gotten used to be being told that I was a courageous and inspiring figure. I had started to believe it myself.

"Meghan, go to hell. You weren't there."

"In fact, I *was* there. I was trying to help other people get away, or not get eaten, or crushed, or electrocuted by that crashing light tower, or shot by idiots with guns. That's what some of us were doing, Nate."

"I meant – jeez, I couldn't make it shoot anyway."

"Hello – guns have safeties on them? Because they are dangerous?"

Meghan also pointed out that there were cops in the stadium who, seeing me brandishing a gun, could have arrested me or done much worse, seeing that they knew perfectly well how to operate their sidearms. After she had reamed me back and forth on this subject a few times, I decided not to tell anyone else about the gun fiasco.

Meanwhile everything, especially my chest and shoulder, either itched or hurt like hell. When an orderly came in to take me for a walk, I was already sitting on the edge of my bed, gingerly putting slippers on while managing an IV drip. He took my arm as I stood up.

"Dizzy?" he asked.

"No. I'm fine." Sam and Mehri appeared in the doorway. I thought fast.

"Maybe a bit dizzy," I said. "But my friends are here. They can help me."

"When I came here before," Sam said, "you were totally out of it."

"Here, you guys, help me down the hall." I put an arm around Sam, and one around Mehri. "Can you get that, Sam?"

Sam took charge of the IV and we made our way down the hall past patients and visitors. I was thinking about how terrific it felt to lean up against Mehri. Her left deltoid, under my cupped hand, felt just great, and so did resting my arm on her shoulders and the back of her neck. Her right arm, which she had curved behind my back with her hand hooked into my hospital gown, was also a perfect fit.

The three of us made small talk as we walked to the end of the hall and back.

"I'm sure glad you guys came," I said. "Now that I'm starting to think about all this stuff, instead of just sleeping all the time, it's depressing."

"I've gone past the church a couple of times," Sam said. "There's never anyone there."

"We actually stopped them," Mehri said. "I think. There have been no more midnight games."

"It's really my dad," I admitted. "I wish he hadn't done that. Took the runes from me, and led the Hounds to himself."

Sam said, "I can't believe what you're saying."

"In fact, if I hadn't gone to that first midnight game, and poked into the cult, none of this would have happened."

"Nate," Mehri took a deep breath, "I can't get my head around everything that's happened. I didn't mean to get involved either. I made one or two decisions, and next thing I knew there was no turning back. But we all know that something very bad was happening – with the Proprietor, and the midnight games, and the Resurrection Church of the Ancient Gods – and that we ruined their plans. We totally messed them up. We might even have saved some innocent people. Maybe a lot of people, because something monstrous was trying to break through – I saw it in the sky, at the ceremony – and somehow, because of what we did, and what your friend Lovecraft did, and the Underground, we helped to stop it."

"Well…" I had wanted to turn my back on all of this, but Mehri was nudging my interest "there was something else too."

"Yes, those horrible centipede monsters … what did they call them?"

"Dritches," I said. "They called them dritches. But I didn't mean that." I told her about the bursts of flame that had repelled Yog-Sothoth, and the airship I had seen erupting from the sky before the continuum threshold had closed. "I saw its name. When the Interlocutor told me that the sorcerer was not a person, but a thing, she didn't mean it was an alien. *Sorcerer* is some sort of huge dirigible-airship thing."

"I saw Yog-Sothoth," Mehri said. "But I didn't see anything like what you're describing."

"I was really close to it. It flickered into view, and then banked over the stadium and headed north. As it did that, it flickered out of sight. So I think if it had some sort of cloaking technology that was acting up."

"I didn't see it," Sam said. "We were trying to avoid those hounds, not looking at the sky. And of course, help people whenever we could. *Sorcerer.* What would an airship – crappy twentieth-century technology – have to do with a distant planet, and interdimensional fissures, and Yog-Sothoth, and the Hounds?"

I shrugged, and suddenly I wasn't faking it. I really did need their help to keep standing. "Jeez, I don't know. I don't know anything. All I know is … I'm going back to bed. And I know that my father is dead."

Sam and Mehri exchanged looks. "What do you mean?"

I collapsed on the side of the bed. "I looked, but I couldn't even find his body. The Hounds completely annihilated any trace … What?" They were staring at me.

"Nate, your father's not dead. He's right down the hall."

"We stopped and said hi to him," Mehri added, "like, ten minutes ago."

CHAPTER 28
RESURRECTION

When Sam had said that he and his family had been in the stadium trying to "help people whenever we could," he thought I knew what he was talking about.

Dad was propped up with tubes in his nose. His chest was bandaged, and he was lying very still, and looking old. But his eyes were lively, and his hands warm as he clasped mine.

"I was so worried about you," he croaked.

"I wasn't worried about you, because I thought you had been killed, and was therefore dead." Dad and I had a big laugh over this as Sam and Mehri eyed us warily. I suppose this says something about where I get my sense of humour.

"When they came at me," Dad explained, "those hounds, some cop pulled out his weapon and took a shot at them. Well whoever this guy was, he shot me instead."

"Uh, what an idiot," I said, inwardly cringing at the memory of my own pathetic gunmanship.

"Not his fault, Nate," Mehri said. "It turns out that bullets go right through the Hounds of Tindalos."

"Cut this poor dude some slack," Dad added. "Ironically, he saved my life. I figure what happened was, the bullet went right through the hound that was about to jump me – so it turned and jumped *him*. I got hit in the chest and went down like a sack of bricks. Another second, and the hound would have ripped me to pieces."

"Remember, Nate, everything happened so fast ..." Sam explained.

I said, "It seems like we were there for hours."

"... the Hounds appeared, then the threshold, then the turf itself opened up beneath our feet and those centipede monsters started popping up everywhere. But once they appeared, the Hounds disappeared almost immediately."

"That's because I was dead," Dad continued.

"What?"

"When I got shot and fell to the ground, my heart stopped. The Hounds were raising hell everywhere else – but when their target died, that's me, their mission was over. They folded up and disappeared into whatever hellish netherworld they come from. Then I guess your friends showed up."

Mehri shrugged. "We just stopped the bleeding and did first aid."

"Yeah," Sam said. "Basic CPR. The paramedics showed up like a second later. It was no big deal."

"It was a big deal for me," Dad said.

"You guys," I said.

"You don't need to … well, just this once," said Sam. I gave him a big hug, and then Mehri.

"You would've done the same thing," Sam said. "Jeez, Nate, you don't have to get all weepy."

CHAPTER 29
A MESSAGE FROM THE BORDER LANDS

By the way, back in grade five, Kara was right; there *was* a knife in my backpack. And a fork. The knife was a dinner knife with a round tip and a blunt serrated edge. In case dessert was in order, there was also a spoon.

Fridays when Dad got paid, I would take the bus after school and meet him at the Lime Ridge Mall food court. We would each have the dinner of our choice, only with the added luxury of our own metal utensils instead of the food court's plastic ones. For me, as I was growing up, this little ritual seemed like haute cuisine and I think Dad enjoyed it too. Okay, okay already, I know it sounds lame, but we thought it was cool.

This was one of the memories that came to me as I lay between the sheets in my own bed, while I tried to will myself to sleep. I hadn't slept well since coming home from the hospital. Dad was still there, but he would be home soon. When I needed someone to pick me up, I had to call on Meghan. I hadn't figured out yet if we were friends, or if we just shared some experiences most people didn't share. She was staying over, sleeping in our spare room; a social worker was due to call tomorrow and Meghan had agreed to pose as my cousin and live-in caretaker.

On the phone, social services had mentioned foster care, a horrifying proposition in which, if Dad turned out to be too disabled, I would go live with some kindly family of complete strangers.

"Why the hell would I want to do that?"

"What you want has nothing to do with it," Meghan explained. "You're still a minor, Nate. Legally, social services can't leave you caring for your father."

I gave Meghan a list of alternatives – selling the house and using the money to get an apartment and some help for dad, quitting school and getting a job, intimidating the social worker with empty threats of horrific violence, but Meghan shot them all down.

"I'm glad to pick you up from the hospital," she said, "and stay over for a day or so, but that's it. Besides, soon your dad will get home. Your life will be normal."

NORMAL, SHE said. In fact, I couldn't claim a genuine night's sleep since that first midnight game, when Dana and I had seen the dritch burst out of the stadium entrance onto Ivor Wynne's field. I thought of Dana, his crosswords, the small talk we tossed back and forth when we met on the street, and his life without family or real friends except for people like me. I thought about the Shirazis, forced halfway around the world by the thugs and creeps who push their way into power wherever there is power to be had, and how they had not been beaten down – "you will go hungry tonight," Mr. Shirazi had said as he put himself in harm's way to save me, when he had his own children to worry about. I thought about the Interlocutor, who was not allowed to choose sides, but she had done so anyway. I thought about this bizarre new world of creatures pushed across space by need and greed and desire, daring countless cold light years of airless dark to get to our world. The weird thing was, whether I wanted to be or not, I seemed to be part of this new world. "Nate Silva," the Interlocutor had said, "you may find that you are a border creature too."

Dad was lucky to be alive, and so was I. We would take things one day at a time. Meanwhile, as long as the *Spectator* kept coming to the front door, I kept updating my scrapbook of clippings. The last midnight game was shrouded in mystery: at fault was a no-account cult whose headquarters in a derelict chain warehouse was now silent and empty. A riot, and explosion, had damaged the stadium so badly that no more football games would ever be held there. Moreover, all this had happened in the midst of a tremendous thunderstorm that had knocked out power for miles around. The cult's leader, Raphe Therpens, had fallen, or been blown, or pushed, from the rim of the stadium onto bare asphalt and had suffered permanent injuries.

Today's sports section had a new article on Ivor Wynne Stadium. The Tragically Hip would play one last concert there, and then it would be demolished, rebuilt and renamed. It would come back bigger and better than ever someday, just like the Ticats, just like the steel industry, just like the city of Hamilton itself. I turned the page and saw an ad for a new condo/office tower to be built downtown. Fifty stories high, it would be the tallest building in the city's history: "sound and solid as our past; soaring as high as our vision of the future." I would have passed it by, if my eye hadn't caught one of the logos in the corner of the page. There it was, among other corporate sponsors.

And the tower's proud name: *Resurrection*.

I looked at the ad and sighed. To hell with it: if the Church was making a comeback, someone else could deal with them. Maybe Daredevil, sick of New York's high rents, would move to Hamilton, or better yet Doctor Strange. I went back to bed and for the first time in days I fell asleep, and didn't dream of death and blood and monsters; didn't dream about unearthly tentacles stretching across the bone-cracking cold of interstellar space. I just fell asleep, and I didn't dream at all, and when I woke up light was coming through the windows. Meghan was gone and I fretted for a moment: the social worker was coming in an hour. Then I saw the text on my phone: *gone to Karlik Pastry for cheese buns, back soon.* The phone was ringing.

Not my cellphone – the kitchen land line, soon to be discontinued, with Dad on disability and the only incoming calls from cruise vacations and phony public service organizations, and Uncle Don. My cellphone would do me. But still sleepy, I stumbled downstairs, picked up the receiver and heard a woman's voice.

"Gord?"

"No, it's not Gord," I grumbled. "Gord is my father. He is presently indisposed." It had been ten days now since the final game. Pretty much everyone who knew my dad had come to Hamilton General to see him. Who the hell was this?

"Oh," the woman gasped. "So it's true. We've had the radio on, but I couldn't believe it … but, Nate, this is you? You sound so *grown-up*!"

The voice sounded familiar, but I couldn't conjure a face to go with it. "Who is this?"

"I can't see you just yet," the woman said. "It's complicated. I need to tell your father; I've left something there. If you haven't found it already. There's a trip I wanted you both to take. I've hidden a package …" She started telling me about the hiding place of this alleged package.

"What trip?" I asked. "Because Dad's not here; if anyone's taking a trip, it'll be me."

"No not you, honey," she said. "Not yet. Not 'til you're older."

"Up yours, lady. I'm sixteen," I said. Satisfyingly, she gasped in shock, but what did I care? Clearly, this was some Resurrection Church nutcase trying to get at me for their own screwed-up reasons. I thought of what the Interlocutor had said as she thrust herself between me and those creeps from the Church. "And he is never a kid again."

"This kid thing is getting old. Who the hell are you to tell me anything?"

She started to tell me who she was, but I cut her off. Now I was getting really mad.

"And another thing. We won, you lost. *Comprenez-vous*? The Resurrection Church of the Ancient Gods is finished and defunct. You stupid loser and liars and pissheads think Yog-

Sothoth is coming? Well he's not ... not on my watch. We had him crying for mercy."

"Actually," she said, "that was us."

"I stopped him once, and I will stop him again. If you keep bugging me, I will hunt down every one of you and I will hurt you. I am Nathan Stefano Silva ..."

"I kn-know you are ..." she stuttered. "I ..."

"... and you have made a big mistake, getting on my bad side. I will find the *Sorcerer* ..."

"You don't understand. I was *on* the *Sorcerer*..."

"... and I will burn it to the ground and piss on its ashes. Or I will board it like a goddamn pirate, with my pirate friends –" I was really mad, but I was enjoying being mad. "– and take it over, and destroy Cthulhu, and smash Yog-Sothoth, and blow up the bridge between worlds for good, and I will hurt the Resurrection Church so bad, that it will never resurrect. Everything, all the brutal fascist crap you believe in, that will be ashes too for me to piss on."

"But, Nate!"

"Do not call this number again."

I slammed the phone down and then knocked it off the counter. It crashed to the floor. I picked it up and pulled the cord out. There was other stuff on the counter – flyers, a cutting board, an old CD player – that I felt like smashing, but I knew I had to calm down.

I could hear Meghan coming back from the bakery. I went out the back door and into the yard where I threw the phone into the bamboo. If there was another dritch growing there, it would have to learn who was boss around here.

Then I flopped down onto the porch step. I sat there and the autumn wind bit hard through my pyjama pants and T-shirt. I shivered, and saw Rocky's black head stick up eagerly over the fence. A hole gaped in our bamboo patch where the dritch had sprouted and grown. Would it be back? Or had all the dritches, every last one of them, returned to their world? Was Rocky in danger? Maybe he knew more about all this than he could tell me. Anyway, I had the feeling I would find out more, whether I wanted to or not. Maybe when the stars were aligned, or when the worlds came together again, or when forces started up that I couldn't begin to understand, much less predict.

Meghan came out onto the porch behind me, carrying a bag of cheese buns. "What was that all about?"

"It's those creeps from the Church," I said. "They piss me off. They won't leave us alone. I told them I would kick their asses." I laughed bitterly. "Hope they don't take me up on it!"

"Where's the phone?"

"I dropped it. Yeah, some Resurrection Church clown phoned. They are such losers. One of them phoned, pranking me. She said –"

Suddenly I was breathless, running out of anger, feeling again that I had just got out of bed and was only half in the real world, still half dreaming.

"– she said that she was my mother."

ACKNOWLEDGEMENTS

Thanks to Mandie at Magicuts for steering me to the story of Evelyn Dick (who, it turns out, lived just a few blocks from my house, in the neighbourhood where the events of this book unfold). Thanks to Beverley Daurio and Maureen Cochrane for reading and responding to the manuscript at crucial junctures. Thanks to Hasti Havari Nasab for her advice on Persian culture. Please bear in mind that whenever I have been given common-sense advice with this book, I have tended to take it wherever I wanted it to go. As a result, any errors of fact, or judgement, that appear in this book are solely the author's responsibility.

David Neil Lee is the author of the west coast novel *Commander Zero*, and the non-fiction books *The Battle of the Five Spot: Ornette Coleman and the New York Jazz Field*, *Stopping Time: Paul Bley and the Transformation of Jazz* and the international bestseller *Chainsaws: A History*. He is also a double bassist who performs with poet/musicians such as Gary Barwin and Arthur Bull, and has toured and recorded with Leo Smith, Joe McPhee, as well as the Canadian group the Bill Smith Ensemble. Originally from British Columbia, David has lived with his family in Hamilton, Ontario, since 2002. Visit his website at www.davidneillee.com.

David Neil Lee is the author of the short story novel *Commander Zero* and the non-fiction books *The Battle of the Five Spot: Ornette Coleman and the New York Jazz Revolution* (Mercury Press, 2006) and *The Midnight Games* (Wolsak and Wynn). He is also a double bassist who, working with poets/musicians such as Steve Dalachinsky and Arthur Bull, and has founded and toured and with Leo Smith, Joe McPhee, as well as the duplex group The Bill Smith Ensemble. Though from British Columbia, David Lee lived with his family in Hamilton, Ontario, since 2004. Visit his website at www.davidneillee.com.